- HARRIS COUNTY PUBLIC LIBRARY

Mystery Watts X
Watts, Larry
Murder on the seawall

$9.26
ocn952335716
First edition.

MURDER ON THE SEAWALL

Third in the

Tanner & Thibodaux Series

Larry Watts

MURDER ON THE SEAWALL

A Tanner & Thibodaux Crime Novel

Copyright © January 2015 by Larry Watts

First edition October, 2015

ISBN-13: 978-1512280494

ISBN-10: 1512280496

All rights reserved. No part of this publication may be reproduced, stored in retrieval system, or transmitted, in any form or by any means, electronic, mechanical, photocopy, recording, or otherwise, without the written permission of the author.

This is a work of fiction. All characters and events depicted herein are fictional and the product of the author's imagination.

Special thanks to my partner, fellow author, editor and inspiration, Carolyn Ferrell Watts.

This book is dedicated to one of my four editors, Gloria Hander Lyons, who passed from this earth after editing was complete and before publication.

I also want to thank Rene Palmer Armstrong and Tom Rizzo for their advice and editing.

Chapter 1

Sanford Hill made a U-turn and parked his Maserati on the Galveston seawall nearly a mile west of 61st Street. His was the only vehicle in sight at three o'clock in the morning. He got out and began walking east, the direction from which he came. Sanford enjoyed the solitude of late night walks looking out on the Gulf waters.

Pausing just a few feet from the Maserati, he stretched and breathed deeply of the Gulf breeze gusting toward the island, accompanied by white-foamed waves that pounded the sand fifteen feet below at the bottom of the Seawall. A spray of salt water moistened Sanford's face; he smiled at the familiar salty taste on his lips. Even as a boy he'd enjoyed this moonlit view of the swirling waters of the mighty Gulf of Mexico, its white-capped waves rushing in with the tide. He could barely detect lights of a distant ship passing.

The sound of a vehicle approaching broke the mood; Sanford turned to look. A pick-up truck pulled to a stop beside him. The driver lowered the passenger window and scooted across the seat.

"What the hell are you doing out here?" Sanford asked.

Without a word, the occupant raised a pistol and shot him in the face. As Sanford fell, two more shots were fired into his body before the shooter returned to the driver's position and sped away. The roar of the surf was the only sound Sanford Hill heard as life seeped slowly from his body.

Because the rumble of the tide water rushing in and receding had muted the sound of gunshots, the lack of traffic at the early morning hour, and the distance to the nearest condominium project, almost two hours passed before a jogger discovered the body and called police. When they arrived and recognized the victim, the senior officer placed a call to Chief of Police Henry Barsetti.

He answered on the first ring, "Barsetti."

"Chief, this is Officer Thomas. We're at a murder scene out on the west end of the seawall. Thought you'd want to know. The victim is Sanford Hill. Appears he was shot at least three times."

"You got a suspect or any witnesses?"

"No one except for the jogger who found the body. Detectives are on the way, but we figured it being Hill, we should call you."

Chief Barsetti hung up and prepared for a busy day. Sanford Hill owned Hill and Sons Industries. His father, Sanford Hill Sr., started the company forty years earlier. The elder Hill had been a welder with a small shop. He soon expanded into repairing shrimp boats and other equipment. Later, he seized an opportunity to build a single barge for use on the ship channel to Houston. This business quickly expanded to include nearly any industrial manufacturing that might be needed along the coast, including tanks, water towers and other equipment used in the petrochemical industry. When Sanford Sr.

died five years earlier, he had built a multi-billion dollar business. Sanford Jr. took the reins of the company.

Barsetti expected Sanford's mother would demand an arrest before the end of the day. The Chief didn't look forward to dealing with her regarding the investigation of her son's murder. Molly B, as most referred to her, was a character in her own right.

Before the Chief left his office for the day, investigators identified several potential suspects, but no evidence. They also assembled a long list of residents in the vicinity of the murder who would be interviewed in the coming days. At eight o'clock that evening, thirty minutes after he arrived home, there was a knock at his door. He opened it and motioned Captain Chad Browning into the house.

Browning followed Barsetti into a den decorated with sailing ship models, old nautical gear and paintings of some of Galveston's several historical buildings. The Chief invited his long-time friend to sit in one of two large leather chairs strategically placed to allow the occupants a sense of intimacy when they conversed.

Both men were born on the island and grew to adulthood together. There was a fraternity that was not hampered by rank or social status as the two men talked.

"Any progress?"

"Not much, Henry. Family's not functioning well, as you might expect. I talked with Molly B late this afternoon. She's convinced Sanford's ex-girlfriend killed him. Her name is Ginger Breedlove. She's got a solid alibi though, been at a real estate conference in

Dallas for three days and won't be back until tomorrow."

"Yeah, Molly B called for me twice today and again a few minutes after I arrived home, but I avoided her until I could talk with you and get more information. I'll call her back tomorrow. Who else is on the short list of suspects?"

"Nobody who sticks out like a sore thumb, but there are three other potentials. Bobby Brown, the business agent for the longshoremen's union has been battling with Sanford and the other Port Commissioners for months. No reason to believe that it's heated up recently, but we're checking.

"And of course, everyone knows about the bad blood between Sanford, Jr. and the entire Scardino family. They've never forgiven him for divorcing Theresa and leaving her with two kids to raise. She's got to be on the list, along with her two brothers. The rumor is that they've all three continued to harbor anger toward him even though the divorce was settled several years ago. We'll check all three out.

"Finally, there's Sanford's sister, Michelle, and her husband, Donny Dragna. No indication that they were unhappy when Molly B turned the business over to Sanford after her husband's death. Furthermore, I don't see Donny as a guy who would have the stomach for murder, but I want to be sure we at least rule them out."

"Stay on it Chad. Molly B's going to be a pain in the ass until this is resolved," Barsetti said, as he walked the Captain to the door.

*****

Three months after the murder, detectives had little to show for their efforts. All potential suspects offered solid alibis. No convincing evidence existed to tie them to the crime. Ginger Breedlove and the Dragnas were all but eliminated as possible suspects. Breedlove because of her solid out of town alibi and the Dragnas simply because there was no known motive.

Chief Barsetti sat in his office, locked in eye contact with Molly B Hill, who sat across from him. He'd known her since he was a small child. He remembered her then as a friendly woman who always had time to talk to children and later, in his teen years as an attractive, somewhat flirty, pretty woman whose visage sometimes invaded his late night teenage thoughts as he lay in bed.

But as she sat across the table this day, she was an old but spirited woman. Had he not known her all his life he might have pitied the woman with a face leathery from too much sun and coastal wind. The grief shown on her face just as it had every time he'd seen her since her son's funeral. Her voice, however, reminded the Chief that there was more than grief residing below the surface of outward appearance.

"Henry, I want to know when your boys are going to arrest that slut, Ginger Breedlove, for murdering my son. It's been three months. Time to do your job."

Barsetti wouldn't be bullied. "You know we don't have any reason to arrest her. She was out of town when Sanford was murdered. They hadn't been dating for several months before his death."

"But she always had designs on his money. He broke up with her because he recognized she was just after status and wealth. She never loved him."

Molly B leaned forward, as if to make a point. "Henry, I supported your appointment as Chief of Police when others said you were too controversial. You've proven that I was right, at least up until now. If you won't make the arrest, I'll have our security team bring in someone to help you prove she did this."

As she stood to leave, Barsetti stood behind his desk. It was true that when he was being considered for the position of police chief, some thought he was too much of a rogue cop. He'd been involved in three shootings and; although cleared in every one, his appointment had not been easy. The night of the vote by Galveston's City Council, Molly B had appeared to speak in favor of the appointment in her usual bombastic manner. The vote was unanimous.

Obvious compassion didn't show often on Barsetti's strong, chiseled face, but strong matriarchs had a special place in his heart. Just hearing her determination triggered memories of how his mother dealt with the unexpected death of her husband. The Chief and his two brothers had met before their father's funeral and discussed how they would care for their mother as they had witnessed their father do for so many years.

But the widow Barsetti surprised them all. A week after the funeral she visited with her husband's lawyer, banker and real estate agent. By the second week she had a grasp on the new responsibility of handling her financial affairs and varied real estate interests. It was soon clear to the three brothers that she, like Molly B, would now take control of her own destiny. He admired both women, but that did not prevent him from offering one tidbit of advice to the grieving mother of Sanford Hill.

"Molly B, don't waste your money. Whoever killed Sanford will be caught. You just can't assume that you know who the killer is without some evidence."

She gave him a withering glare before turning to leave the office.

Chapter 2

Calvin Thibodaux rolled onto his side facing the body of the woman who slept soundly in his bed. Slowly, he caressed the small of her back as she lay curled in a semi-fetal position. As he moved his hand around her body and touched her breast, she stirred slightly before turning toward him, stretching, and awakening slowly. He loved her emerald green eyes. They reminded him of his niece, Danielle, whose murder two years earlier, was constantly just below the surface of his conscious thought. Marissa also shared the same olive-toned skin of his niece.

He leaned down and kissed her lips, continuing the exploration of her body with his fingertips. She reciprocated and soon they were passionately pounding against each other's bodies as if both had been deprived of such pleasure for a long time. In fact, they had made love just a few hours earlier.

Later, Thibodaux lay next to her thinking that he had never expected he could be so in love with a woman. Through a career in the Army as a member of the Delta Force, he never surrendered to love. He'd sampled the fruits of feminine sexuality all over the world without the need for emotional attachment. But Marissa Carmona was different.

Thibodaux's cell phone began vibrating before it rang. He reached for it on the nightstand beside the bed.

"Hello."

"Cal? Is that you," a vaguely familiar voice pulled him from his thoughts of love. Who was it? No one had called him Cal since he left the Army's Delta Force and retired to his home town.

"Yeah, this is Calvin Thibodaux. Who's this?"

"Johnny Blackman. Man who saved your ass from those two Navy Seals in that bar in Panama."

"Johnny! What's going on man? Where are you? It's been years."

The two old friends had met while stationed in Panama after the capture of Manuel Noriega. Their station assignments had been parallel for most of the rest of their careers. Johnny retired two months after Thibodaux.

"I'm in Galveston. Landed a job leading a small security detail for a company here. Hill and Sons Industries is the name. How about you? I know you went back home to a small town in central Texas. Success, that's the name of the town, right?"

Thibodaux watched as Marissa left the bed, stretched, accentuating her nakedness, and strode to the shower. Although distracted, Thibodaux tried to keep his focus on the conversation. He told his old friend about having come home with plans of operating a small landscaping business and how those plans changed when his niece was murdered. Milo Tanner and Thibodaux had teamed up to solve the case. The relationship grew into a full-time private investigations business.

Johnny listened with interest until Thibodaux paused, then he spoke.

"That's why I'm calling. I've got a case I want you to work on here in Galveston. My boss, Sanford Hill, was murdered a few months ago. Police can't seem to put a case together on the prime suspect. Mrs. Hill, Sanford's mother, wants me to hire someone to make sure she gets justice for her son."

Thibodaux's reaction was one of caution. In his new career, he learned early that justice is sometimes elusive. He'd rather stay right here in Success and enjoy his new-found love.

"Johnny, I'm sure you can find someone in the Galveston area for this. What I didn't tell you is that I've met a woman. She owns a nursery and landscaping business here in town. When I was landscaping, I bought my supplies from her. About the only thing left of the nice, quiet, peaceful retirement I envisioned is when I can hang out with her helping in the nursery business."

"Sorry, Cal, but I can't take no for an answer. Molly B Hill is the dead man's mother and she's convinced you and your partner are the only people who can make sure the murderer doesn't get away.

"Hell, I didn't recommend you, didn't even know you were in the business. She called around before she told me what she wanted to do. She heard about you guys. I think it was some business acquaintance of hers in San Antonio who gave her your names. You guys helped him with a case in which his son was murdered.

"At any rate, I need you to come visit with her. Don't make a decision until after that. And bring your new partner with you. I look forward to meeting him."

Thibodaux preferred sitting in front of his computer performing skip-traces for people who skipped out on debt or occasionally for a wanted fugitive with a bounty on his head. But he knew, since he and Tanner worked on two previous murder cases, that Tanner would want to make the trip to Galveston and probably take the case. His partner didn't have anyone in his life.

It was Sunday morning. Thibodaux regretted leaving Marissa. They had planned to visit her nursery to water plants and spend time in the cool freshness of one of the greenhouses. Thibodaux thought of the experience as therapeutic, similar to losing himself in a rain forest. Far better than spending time with a professional counselor or a psychologist.

When he walked into Tanner's home, the strong aroma of freshly-brewed coffee permeated the air. Five minutes after he arrived, the two men sat on the front porch sipping the dark brew as Thibodaux told him about the phone call from Galveston.

"Good," Tanner replied as his friend finished. "I'm getting bored with the routine work we've been doing. I know the police chief there. He and I worked a case or two when we were detectives. It'll be a good chance to renew the acquaintance."

"Well, just for the record, I'd as soon stay here and do the boring work," Thibodaux said.

"Sure you would, partner. You're getting serious about Marissa. It's been obvious for months now. I don't blame you though. She's a winner."

Thibodaux finished his coffee and left. He drove straight to Marissa's nursery and found her trimming leaves from small trees growing in large pots. She didn't hear him as he walked up behind her. He paused and admired her lean athletic body as she leaned over to pick a leaf off the floor. He was amazed at the feelings he experienced simply by being near this woman as he stepped forward and engulfed her body in his arms.

"Let's start again where we left off this morning," he suggested as Marrissa struggled to turn and face him.

She smiled and reached to place the pruning knife on a table. Both hands went to his cheeks and she held his face like a mother would hold a son.

"I'll bet you're going to tell me you have another case that will take you out of town again. When you get Sunday morning calls, I know it's either that or you have some little chickadee on the side I don't know about."

Thibodaux shared the information about the murder case his old Army buddy wanted him to investigate. One of the things he loved about Marissa was that she was interested in his work.

"Here's my proposition to you, Mr. Thibodaux. Let's go back to your place and resume our love making, but you have to promise me two things. First, that if you take the job in Galveston, we'll schedule a long weekend there with all your attention on me."

"Done," Thibodaux chuckled as he spoke. "What's the second promise?"

"That you'll leave your cell phone in the living room when we get to your house," she said as she took his hand, leading him out of the greenhouse.

Chapter 3

As Tanner drove through the late morning traffic in Houston, he thought how much less frustrating it was to weave in and out of bumper-to-bumper commuter traffic now that it was not a daily routine. With Thibodaux riding shotgun, they were soon speeding south out of town, headed for Galveston Island, just fifty miles farther.

They arrived at the old red brick industrial building that faced Harborside Drive nearly thirty minutes before their scheduled one o'clock meeting. Johnny Blackman met them just inside the entrance to the office section of the building. After a quick introduction of Tanner and Johnny, as well as a promise by Thibodaux to spend time catching up with each other's lives later, Johnny ushered them into Molly B's office.

She was a small woman, about five foot two, and still attractive though she was probably past eighty years old. She held a thin cigar in her left hand as she extended her right to Thibodaux.

"You must be the Army buddy. He said you were black. I guess he thought that made a difference."

She turned slightly toward Tanner and shook his hand as well.

"Have a seat," Molly B said, motioning toward a small table with four chairs." Tanner thought her rapid breathing, tightly pursed lips and gravelly voice belied her attempt to maintain strength and controlled emotions. "My boy was murdered by a woman who wanted to marry him, or she hired somebody to do it. I want her punished for that. I'm told you two are the team who can make it happen.

"Johnny can give you the details. I'll pay you without objection as you submit your bills. Any questions?"

Tanner looked at Thibodaux briefly and then turned back to face her.

"Mrs. Hill, I think…"

"It's Molly B. No formality here. I grew up in a whorehouse on Post Office Street, back when whorin' was a respectable occupation in Galveston. Married Sanford Hill when he was still runnin' numbers out of the Balinese Room on the pier. So what's your question?" Her back seemed to stiffen as she looked squarely into Tanner's eyes.

Tanner smiled slightly, "Well, since you are convinced you know who ordered your son's murder, you're going to need to tell us how you know that. Seems to me if the case was that clear cut, there might already have been an arrest."

Before she could respond, Thibodaux added, "Besides that, we haven't said we're interested in the case. You may call it an open and shut case, but we need more information before we make that decision."

Molly B turned slightly to study the strong, steady gaze and calm demeanor of the retired military man. "We're going to get along just fine, boys. Maybe I was a little abrupt. I know people. Been studying 'em all my life," she said, pausing, her eyes trailing left and downward, as if following a memory. "Used to hide under the staircase and try to figure out which of the johns that came into Millie's Parlor were going to be the big tippers and which ones she'd have to throw out for not treating her girls right."

Molly B glared into empty space, clinching her teeth, she began to shake her head slightly, then spoke softly but firmly.

"So I knew, when my son started bringing that Ginger Breedlove around, exactly what she was. I told him after the first time I met her not to bring her back. I can smell a money-grubber a mile away. He stopped dating her and look what it got him. Deader'n Hell." She looked each of the men straight in the eyes, her lips pressed hard together, as she released a deep breath.

"So, what do the police say about her being a suspect?" Tanner asked.

"She was out of town, so they stopped looking at her right away. Henry Barsetti is a good cop, but he don't know people like I do. I want you two to make the connection and hand the case to him. I will have justice for my boy."

"By the way," Thibodaux added, "I see your company's name is Hill and Sons. Does that mean there are other children?"

"We have a daughter. She's the youngest. Sanford was first. Our second son died the day after he was born. I made Sanford name the company 'and Sons' so we'd never forget that little boy. And I haven't."

"Daughter involved in the business?" Tanner asked.

"Her husband is the company accountant. She owns part of the company, as did Sanford, Jr. So what's it going to take to get you boys started?"

"We'll visit with Johnny and let you know," Thibodaux replied. "But you need to know, if we work for you, we go where the evidence leads us, regardless of your notion about who's guilty."

The two men stood and both looked at Johnny Blackman, who was standing behind Molly B with a grin on his face. He ushered them out of the office and back to the entrance.

When they were on the sidewalk, Johnny chuckled and said, "I'll say this for you two. You handled Molly B about as well as anyone ever does. She's a character and she'll overwhelm you if she can."

"But what's the story on the girlfriend? You think she was involved in the son's murder?" Tanner asked.

"Not a clue, but they hadn't been dating for some time and I thought they'd both moved on with their lives. I don't keep up with her love life, but I know she's out and about with other guys. Sanford was playing the field again, but I always thought that she broke up with him. If that is what happened, I don't see her holding a grudge. Molly B may be letting her anger about his death cloud her judgment. But that's for you guys to figure out."

Tanner knew his partner would be happy to reject taking the case, even for his old army buddy. It was two hundred miles from home and would require a lot of time on the Island. But he wanted it. He was bored with the routine P.I. work they had been doing. Besides, he knew he would love listening to the old woman talk about her life, even if she was a little pushy. He decided to make the call without privately consulting Thibodaux.

"So here's the deal, Johnny. We'll take the case with the following stipulations. We stay at the San Luis Hotel when we're in town. Separate rooms and Thibodaux's friend's expenses are included with ours. That includes meals and travel when she has to fly. Those expenses will be direct bill through the company.

"We take this wherever it goes, even if it leads to the old woman herself. If those terms work for you, we're in, if not, we'll head back home."

Thibodaux glared at Tanner. Johnny didn't miss the unspoken communication. He grinned at Thibodaux as he responded.

"Hell, she must be some woman, Cal. It will be worth the cost for her expenses just to see how you act when you're around a woman who has that kind of hold on you." He extended his hand and shook with each man as he said, "Done deal,"

Chapter 4

Tanner and Thibodaux were quiet during the drive down Harborside Drive. The flurry of activity on the docks provided a welcome diversion from their more serious thoughts. A white cruise ship dominated the scene, moored under the hot Texas sun, awaiting new travelers for another seven day cruise.

Piers, lined with colorful shops and restaurants were filled with scattered crowds of tourists and a sprinkling of native Galvestonians. Driving past the Elissa, an old three-mast tall sailing ship reminded Thibodaux of the island's pirate history.

"I've read that Jean Lafitte once ruled this area. I wonder what he would think about today's Galveston."

Tanner enjoyed his partner's interest in history. "My guess is that he would think the island's still a good haven for wild men with French-sounding names. But back to the moment, why don't we spend the night and begin talking with some of the people who might shed light on the murder. We can begin with Chief Barsetti."

While Thibodaux made the arrangements by phone with Johnny Blackman to reserve a couple of rooms at the San Luis, Tanner called the Chief.

After checking into the hotel and finding that Johnny had arranged for a two bedroom suite, the two men sat at the breakfast table with a view of the Gulf of Mexico. They discussed plans for the remainder of the day and decided to try to schedule a couple of interviews before leaving the next day.

Since Tanner had a meeting with the Chief scheduled in less than an hour, Thibodaux agreed to contact Donny Dragna for a meeting. They knew that the finances of Hill and Sons might shed light on a motive. Thibodaux would try to set a meeting for the following morning with the victim's ex-wife, Theresa Scardino, and with Molly B's favorite suspect, Ginger Breedlove. Tanner left him searching for phone numbers.

He drove to the new Law Enforcement Center, where the Galveston Police Department shared a complex with the County Sheriff. Tanner entered the lobby and told the woman seated behind a heavy glass window that he had an appointment with Chief Barsetti. Minutes later a middle-age, attractive woman exited the elevator and approached Tanner.

"Mr. Tanner? I'm Sylvia, Chief Barsetti's assistant. If you'll follow me, the Chief is waiting."

A quick ride in the elevator and Sylvia ushered him into an office where Barsetti sprang to his feet, rounded the desk, holding out his hand in greeting.

"Tanner, you son-of-a-gun. It's good to see you. How long has it been? Ten years or more?"

"At least, ten, Henry. And look at you. I'd have never guessed you'd be sitting in a Chief's office. Congratulations."

"Well, you were a Houston cop. It's too big, so local talent doesn't necessarily rise to the top there. But here in Galveston, just being a Barsetti was good enough to get me considered for the job. I have to admit though, there were some who thought it was a mistake."

The two men took seats at a small conference table as Sylvia walked out of the room and closed the door. The conversation moved quickly to the reason for Tanner's visit.

"I understand Molly B hired you to help me with my job." Barsetti smiled, but the irritation was evident.

"Word travels fast here on the Island I guess. We just met with her an hour ago. Tell me what you can about the case."

"I can tell you that she has an unreasonable obsession about Ginger Breedlove being responsible for her son's death. Ms. Breedlove has an ironclad alibi for the night of the murder. We've also checked her phone records, which she voluntarily allowed, by the way. Nothing there to indicate any connection with Sanford Hill's death. Not on her home phone, business line, or either of her two cell phones.

"Truth is, we're stuck in the mud on this one. No witnesses. No forensic evidence at the scene except for two of the slugs that the medical examiner recovered from the body. Looks like 9mm ammo and both are in good shape if we had a weapon to compare them to, which we don't. That's about it.

"So I welcome your looking this case over, even if I resent Molly B bringing you in. My guys will help you with anything you need from us."

"I appreciate that, Henry. I will say that our new client is quite a character. Is it true that she grew up in a whorehouse?"

"It is. She had a rough life, but she's one of the good ones. She's richer than sin, but you'd never know it. You might see her talking to one of the meth whores on the street from time to time and she thinks nothing of it. Kind of scares most of us who care for her, but she handles herself pretty well. She was also one of my most vocal supporters, when some of the Chamber of Commerce crowd tried to keep me from getting this job."

The two old friends discussed the case, the people, and an assortment of theories about the death for another hour before Tanner said goodbye. When he arrived back at the hotel, Thibodaux told him that they both had meetings set for ten the next morning, Tanner with Ginger Breedlove at her office and Thibodaux back at the offices of Hill and Sons Industries where he would meet Donny Dragna, the company accountant. The ex-wife was out of town. They would schedule a meeting with her on their next trip to Galveston.

With the evening free, they walked down the sidewalk beside the seawall, to the Olympia Grill. Both men enjoyed Greek food and it was a special treat to drink authentic Greek beer with the meal. After a relaxing dinner, they strolled back to their hotel, accompanied by the sounds of the Gulf waters crashing onto the nearly abandoned beach, then receding. Back in their rooms, they changed into bathing suits before meeting at the pool to lounge in deck chairs.

"You think Marissa will enjoy a few days here in Galveston?" Tanner asked.

"I'm sure she will," Thibodaux responded, but he sat back in his chair with a troubled expression.

"You pissed because I told Blackman we'd take the case without talking it over, partner?" Tanner asked.

"No, but I have to tell you, I don't want this case turning into another circumstance where we get caught up in exacting justice ourselves. Being the judge, jury, and executioner doesn't set well with me, even though I know I demanded it when Danielle was murdered."

"Partner, we'll never do anything that we don't both agree is right. When we took care of Danielle's killer, it was right. When we did the work in San Antonio and up in the Davis Mountains, it was the only way to ensure that more young men and boys wouldn't be abused by a sick billionaire with the ability to buy out the justice system. The same applies in this case. Let's see where it leads, but we'll try to stick with just gathering evidence."

They continued to talk for nearly an hour as they sat admiring pelicans soaring overhead, like squadrons of planes in military formation, as white-crested waves crashed onto the shore over and over.

Thibodaux confided to Tanner that his entire life had changed since the developing relationship with Marissa Carmona. He asked Tanner if he'd ever had a relationship that seemed more important than everything else going on in his life. With sadness, Tanner told him he had not, but he was happy for his partner.

Then bounding from his deck chair, Tanner continued, "But I'm an optimist. It's never too late to have good things happen in your life. Let's call it a night."

The two men retired to their rooms, each lost in his own thoughts about life. Tanner was happy for his friend, but he couldn't imagine ever gambling on another relationship with a woman himself. The hurt had been too deep when his marriage had ended.

Policing streets and interacting with the nocturnal underworld of Houston had earned him two shields. The obvious one was pinned on his shirt upon graduation from the police academy. The second shield was more subtle, almost invisible, but hard and impenetrable. It served well as a defense against letting emotions influence his work.

Chapter 5

Up early the next morning, Tanner and Thibodaux drank coffee on the balcony. They would attend their meetings and then rendezvous at the coffee shop in the Holiday Inn a few blocks from their hotel. Since they were in Tanner's car, he dropped Thibodaux in front of the offices of Hill and Sons. When his meeting with Dragna was over, Thibodaux planned to catch a taxi back to the hotel.

The receptionist was expecting Thibodaux and ushered him into Donny Dragna's office immediately. Sitting behind an enormous desk covered with spreadsheets, calculators and a laptop computer was a man whose picture, Thibodaux thought, should be in the dictionary beside the word 'accountant.' He was in his forties, beginning to bald, and wore reading glasses well toward the end of his nose.

Dragna glanced over the glasses, his attention to a spreadsheet interrupted. His facial expression revealed the slight hint of irritation, but a smile replaced it as if from a long practiced habit.

"Mr. Thibodaux. Have a seat. I understand Mom has engaged your services regarding the death of my brother-in-law. I hope I can help you."

"Thanks. I appreciate you having agreed to see me on such short notice. I'm putting together what I call the storyboard about your brother-in-law. It's important to know the people, how they interact, and everything possible that might help to solve the crime.

"What I'd like to understand is the structure of Hill and Sons Industries. I believe Mrs. Hill owns a controlling interest and that Sanford and your wife, Michelle, each owned minority shares. Is that right?"

"Yes, it is. Mom owns a sixty percent share. Michelle and Sanford had equal interest in the remaining forty. Of course, with Sanford's death, when his estate is settled, his children will split his share."

Thibodaux took notes as Dragna spoke. When he stopped, Thibodaux asked, "And what is the financial condition of the company?"

It was obvious from his expression that the son-in-law didn't like the question, but he answered.

"Normally we don't discuss such matters outside the family, but Mom made it clear that I was to answer all your questions.

"The company is in excellent shape financially. We have all the business we can handle. The future is bright; in fact, if Mom decided to take it public, there would be a windfall of profit that would serve to insure the family wealth for several generations."

"And is making a public offering of shares something that has been discussed?" Thibodaux asked.

"From time to time the family has entertained the idea. Mom is open to it. Maybe even more so with Sanford gone. He believed the company should remain solely in the hands of the Hill family."

"As the money-cruncher, what is your opinion?" Thibodaux thought the use of the informal term might irritate Dragna, but there wasn't even a pause.

"My advice has been to go public. But it's purely from a perspective of risk. The family wealth is insured to a greater extent. But I'm an accountant. Mom will tell you that I am adverse to risk. Not so much of an entrepreneurial spirit as the Hill bloodlines have." He smiled as he finished speaking.

"You have any ideas about Sanford's death?"

"I know Mom believes it was his former girlfriend. I don't have a clue. Mom may be right. Sanford could be a really generous guy, but he also had a big ego and could rub people the wrong way. I don't know of anyone who would want to kill him though."

Thibodaux thanked him and ended the meeting. He knew there would be more discussions, but he'd learned enough for now. He asked the receptionist to call a cab for him and waited at the door.

*****

Tanner had been surprised to learn that Ginger Breedlove's offices were in the Moody Bank Building on Post Office Street. He had assumed that she was a residential realtor. But the listing at the elevators was for Breedlove Commercial and Industrial Real Estate. He took the elevator to her floor and found that she had a small, but attractive, corner space with a receptionist.

"Good morning. I'm Milo Tanner. I have an appointment with Ms. Breedlove this morning," he told the receptionist.

He sensed a cold response from the young woman, who simply said, "One moment, please," as she pushed the intercom button on her phone. After a brief conversation, the receptionist pointed to the office behind her. "She'll see you now."

Tanner walked into the office and was greeted by a woman who could have been anywhere from twenty-five to forty-five years old. Although seated behind a desk, she appeared to be a few inches over five feet tall, with beautiful red hair cut in a pageboy style. Vivacious was the word that came to mind as he stared at her.

"Mr. Tanner. I understand the Hills have hired you to try to convince the police to arrest me for murder. I spoke to my attorney this morning. He advised me to cancel the meeting and say nothing more regarding Sanford Hill. Any reason you think I shouldn't follow his advice?" She didn't suggest that he sit.

Tanner realized he was in the presence of a woman who was sure of her capabilities and didn't waste time with southern genteel formalities. He also thought that he now understood the hostility of her secretary. As far as she was concerned, he was trying to send her boss to jail for murder. He liked Ginger Breedlove immediately, but knew that one of the great short-comings of average investigators was to form personal opinions, good or bad, of those they questioned.

"Because you agreed to the appointment, I spent the night in Galveston just to meet with you, and it would be rude to change your mind now." He was sure it worked when he saw the hint of a smile on her lips.

"Sit," she said, gesturing toward one of the chairs facing her desk. "I've cooperated with every request from the police regarding Sanford's death, including my phone and e-mail records and submitting my pistol for testing. What can I tell you that will satisfy the old woman? I didn't kill her son."

Tanner's skills at interrogation and interviews were well-honed, but this blunt and direct lady threw him off, if only a little.

"Who did kill him, if you didn't?" he asked.

"That's not my line of work, but let's see. He has an ex-wife whose kids likely inherit his part of the business, a sister who probably gets control of it now that he's gone, and a half-dozen other ex-girlfriends just like me, who have no reason that I can imagine to have wanted him dead. Sorry, but I don't know who killed him."

"Why'd he break up with you?"

"He didn't. I broke our dating relationship off when I realized that he wasn't the guy I'd want to wake up to every morning for the rest of my life. He was self-centered, used to being pampered by his mother, and just a bad match for me. We broke up on good terms and were both dating again a few weeks later. No hard feelings on either side."

"What kind of pistol do you own?"

"9mm, just like the one used to kill Sanford."

"Can I buy you a cup of coffee across the street?"

The question had no relevance to the direction the conversation had taken to that point. Ginger Breedlove paused before answering. She observed that his questions were as direct and rapid fire as her answers, but the invitation surprised her.

"I don't know where that came from, but yes, let's go get that coffee. I'll just tell my secretary where we'll be, so that if my lawyer calls he can break out in hives when he learns that we've gone for coffee."

Chapter 6

The elevator traveled slowly to the lobby after which the two walked across the street to the cubby-hole of a coffee shop. Tanner's mind dwelt on the word 'methodically', something he always practiced when involved in an investigation. What the hell am I doing, he thought? Why did I invite this woman, who is probably a murderer, to drink a cup of coffee?

When Ginger Breedlove, stepped into the dark coolness of the coffee shop, she smiled thinking how unhappy her lawyer would be with this new development. But she liked this guy Tanner. He wasn't playing games, at least none that she could detect. And she didn't notice the arrogance demonstrated by the police detective who interviewed her earlier.

After ordering coffee, Tanner apologized. "You'll have to forgive me. I don't know why I felt the need to suggest we get out of your office, but it seemed so formal. Thanks for not embarrassing me by declining my invitation. I really do need to ask you more questions."

"I like people who do the unexpected. I didn't expect the private eye who came into my office at the behest of a woman who wants me in prison or worse to suggest we talk over a cup of coffee. So go on. What else can I tell you?"

Ginger was not fearful or intimidated by the fact that Molly B Hill and this detective thought she killed Sanford. She wasn't involved and she was confident that the facts would continue to bear that out.

"If you weren't involved in Sanford's murder, why is Mrs. Hill so adamant that you were?"

"I think that's a better question for her, but I can tell you aside from my not being a BOI, that from the day I first met her, I probably never showed her the deference she has come to expect from those around her."

"BOI?"

Ginger laughed. "Sorry, I forgot that you aren't from the area. BOI means 'born-on-the-island.' That would be Galveston Island and it's a matter of great pride. There's a social structure here that's totally separate from business relationships, fraternal memberships, churches, or groups of other like-minded people. Makes no difference, rich, poor, gay, straight, Italian or Irish, if you're BOI you are in the club.

"It's hard to explain, but some of the older generations still like the idea of keeping BOI bloodlines in their family. Molly B is one of those people. Sanford's first wife, Theresa, is BOI and Michelle's husband Donny Dragna is as well. I'm not and Molly B voiced her displeasure with Sanford when she thought we were a really hot item. She needn't have worried. I would never have married him and he wasn't that interested either."

"Tell me more about why you didn't show her the respect she thought she deserved?" Tanner asked.

"I'm a commercial real estate broker. I've done well for myself in Galveston and I respect the closed culture attitude of those like Molly B who have a romanticized view of what being BOI means. I met Sanford because I had a client who wanted to purchase a piece of land down on the docks that was owned by the Hills. I met Molly B a week or two later after the real estate deal was nearly complete.

"She suggested that I involve another realtor, a guy who flips houses for the most part, to help me with the transaction. I declined to split my fee with her friend, who, by the way, is a BOI." Ginger smiled. "She's not used to being told no by anyone, but especially by a real estate agent from the mainland who she thinks has designs on her son."

The two talked for an hour longer, mostly about the Hill family. As the conversation wound down, Tanner looked thoughtfully into her brown eyes, not quite detecting Ginger's soul, but recognizing the intelligence and accompanying forthrightness. Her eyes softening made his face feel warm and flushed as he realized her amusement at his studied stare.

Knowing well his tendency to retreat from relationship situations, Tanner broke eye contact, taking a deep breath. But laughing at himself inwardly, he stared back into her eyes and with a slight grin said, "I will be back here next week. Will you have dinner with me?"

Once again Ginger greeted the question with what Tanner would come to describe as a mischievously wicked, but beautiful grin. "Does that mean you don't think I'm a murderess?" she asked.

"I'm not sure what it means," Tanner replied, "but, I know if you say yes, it will make my return trip much more enjoyable."

"Then by all means, yes," Ginger said as her expression became very serious. "We must do all we can to ensure that visitors to the Island want to return."

They laughed, Tanner paid the bill, and at the lobby door to the building, he told her he would call when his schedule was worked out. Tanner then drove to the Holiday Inn for his rendezvous with Thibodaux.

*****

He found his partner sitting at a table, sipping from a glass of sweet tea as he watched the waves roll in. Both men were beginning to appreciate the calmness that this phenomenon of nature supplied so freely.

When Tanner was seated, Thibodaux asked, "Well, sir, now that you've interviewed our prime suspect, what do you think?"

"I'm not married to the idea that she's a suspect." He continued nearly too quickly, his face growing more somber. "In fact, I'm becoming more certain that she wasn't involved in Hill's death."

"Now that's an interesting development. How do you know that after spending only a couple of hours with her?" Thibodaux asked, clearly perplexed by the abrupt declaration.

Tanner's face slowly began to flush with embarrassment as he looked at his partner. He peered down at the table and replied, "I'm not absolutely sure, but I'll bet my police pension check she's no murderer."

Thibodaux gazed at Tanner with a questioning expression, but he continued uncomfortably staring at the table. "Partner, have you been hit by one of Cupid's arrows at this late point in life? I've never seen you look so vulnerable."

Tanner suddenly seemed to move beyond the thoughts and embarrassment that he had displayed. Standing, he said, "Come on, let's get on the road. We can discuss the case as we drive."

Hours later, as they passed a sign announcing the city limits of Success, Texas, the two men had discussed their interviews in detail. The case seemed to them, as it did to the police, at a dead-end. But Tanner had one more idea that might break it open.

"We need to find the murder weapon, Tib. That's the only thing that will solve this case."

"How do you propose we do that, my friend? You think the murderer will just respond to a classified ad in the newspaper?"

"No, but we can start with the family. If I convince Molly B we need to eliminate those she has influence with as suspects, she'll make sure we get their weapons. I doubt anyone in the family or on the payroll will be willing to challenge her directive, unless one of them is the murderer."

As they arrived at Thibodaux's home, they decided that he would spend the next week at the computer, compiling research on the family, friends and on Hill and Sons Industries. Tanner would return to Galveston and enlist Molly B's assistance in getting access to as many weapons as possible. He'd let the Chief know of his plans. Although, he'd failed to mention it to Thibodaux, he fully intended to spend another evening with Ginger Breedlove.

As Tanner drove away from his partner's home, he hoped that his intuition was right. He'd never declared a suspect innocent of a crime with such lightning speed. He had also never been so captivated by a woman. For the first time in years, thoughts of enjoying things in life other than work, were taking shape in his mind.

Chapter 7

Monday morning found Thibodaux sitting at his computer researching Hill and Sons Industries. Since it was a privately held corporation, the public information available from governmental agencies was limited. But much could be gleaned from court records, newspaper articles and the social media accounts of employees. He told Tanner he would stay at the computer until early afternoon, when he planned to help Marissa at her nursery.

Tanner called Ginger Breedlove to let her know he would be back in Galveston the next morning. He felt like a teenager when he thought of dinner with her. In fact, he restrained himself from beginning the trip early.

As promised, Thibodaux conducted background checks on Sanford, Mrs. Hill, and Donny Dragna. Although he learned nothing new, he made a list of records he would ask Henry Barsetti to have checked; the ones available only to law enforcement. This included concealed carry permits which the State of Texas had decided would not be made available to the public.

An hour before sunrise, Tanner headed to Galveston. He was early enough to avoid the heaviest of Houston's morning traffic and crossed the Galveston causeway bridge at just before eight. Since his meeting with Mrs. Hill wasn't until eleven, he detoured to the Police Department with his list of requests for the Chief.

Minutes later he sat across from Henry Barsetti explaining what he wanted and why.

"Okay, Tanner. I've already checked on Breedlove, the ex-wife Theresa Scardino, and Sanford Hill himself to see if they had licenses to carry a pistol. Breedlove has one, as did Hill, but Theresa Scardino doesn't. And by the way, I've already had Breedlove's pistol test-fired for comparison. It's not a match."

Tanner knew about the comparison, but kept it to himself. "But will you check the others for me?" he asked.

"Don't you think it's a little over the top to check on Molly B? Surely you don't think she killed her own son and then hired you to prove it."

"No, I don't, but I want all the information I can get, if it's not too much trouble." Tanner knew that one of the failures of good police work was cutting corners. He also knew the Chief would grant his request.

Just after ten, Tanner drove to his meeting with Molly B Hill. He had enjoyed the first meeting with her and was looking forward to this one. Twenty minutes later he walked into her office.

"Tanner, isn't it? Have a seat," Molly B said as he entered the office. "You boys wrapped this up already?"

"Not quite, Mrs....Molly B. I need your help on a couple of things, though. First, do you know where Sanford kept his guns? The second thing I need is for all the family members and employees to let us test any 9mm pistols they own."

"And exactly how does that help prove that the Breedlove girl killed my son," Molly B's expression was as hard as Tanner imagined the old madam at Millie's Parlor had been when she stared at an unruly client.

"Ginger Breedlove is not your son's murderer. If you want an investigation that reaches such a conclusion regardless of facts, then we're finished." Tanner rose as if to leave.

"Sit down, boy." The old woman's tone wasn't harsh, but it was demanding. "Convince me that she's not involved," she said as Tanner lowered himself back into the chair.

Tanner methodically reviewed the evidence, the scrutiny of phone and e-mail records, the testing of Ginger's pistol by police. He also pointed out she had cooperated with the police and with Tanner himself.

Then he added, "I've investigated murders and other crimes for a lot of years. I'm not arrogant about my skills, but I am confident. Don't let the real murderer escape just because you're a hard-headed old woman who has money and expects everyone she knows to agree with her or suffer the consequences."

"Well, kiss my ass and call me darlin'! The last man to talk to me like that who didn't get a pistol shoved in his face ended up marrying me. If I was thirty-five years younger, you'd be in real trouble, son.

"So are you going to catch the person who killed Sanford or are you just trying to run up a high-dollar bill and then tell me you can't make a case on anyone?"

"If you want us to keep looking and if you're willing to trust us and cooperate with everything we ask you to do, we'll identify the killer if it is humanly possible. That's the best assurance I can give you."

"Let's do it then. I told you I know people. I still think that girl was trying to get to Sanford's money, but it didn't happen, so I'll stick with your advice. Hell, the stupidest thing Sanford, Sr. and I ever did was hire a lawyer once to help us settle a lawsuit and then not listen to his advice. Cost a lot of money. But I hired you and Mr. Thibodaux because I was told you're the best, so get to work."

As Tanner stood to leave, he replied, "Don't call him Mister."

"What?" Molly B's quizzical expression was priceless to Tanner.

"Thibodaux. Don't call him Mister. There's no formality around here." Tanner walked out the door, barely concealing a chuckle that started deep in his belly.

He drove to the San Luis, checked in and started unpacking when his phone rang. It was Chief Barsetti.

"I've got your records and a little more. Come by my office when you can."

Tanner was on the road minutes later. He was slowly coming to the realization that he really had been too young to retire. He liked this work! But he relished the freedom from bureaucratic red-tape he now enjoyed as a private investigator. The frustration of having to comply with all the cop rules was long gone.

Chapter 8

It was still early afternoon when he pulled into the parking lot in front of the police station. He would meet with the Chief, then return to the hotel, shower and dress for dinner with Ginger. Fitting the puzzle pieces together during an investigation always kept his interest, but thoughts of the dinner date actually excited him. He smiled inwardly at this nearly forgotten experience.

When he appeared at the receptionist's window, she recognized him and buzzed him through the security door to the elevator. He walked into the Chief's office as Barsetti motioned for him to take a seat.

"So here's what I have for you," Barsetti said, tossing a manila folder across the desk. "Molly B doesn't have a concealed carry permit. Hell, knowing her, she's probably carried a pistol since she was a teenager. She's not one for rules, such as laws that say you can't do things.

"The son-in-law, Donny Dragna, has a permit, but his wife doesn't. A little more info on Donny. One of my detectives told me he and Sanford were regulars at Freedom Rings Firing Range on the mainland, at least every couple of weeks."

"How about Sanford's work on the Port Commission? I understand there was some union trouble. Did your guys check on that?"

"We did. Actually, it's a little strange, but Sanford was aligned with the union on the latest issue, which had to do with how ships were unloaded. We interviewed several people. Got nothing but positive comments about him. My guess is that would be a rabbit trail for you. Our guys aren't playing it as a serious possibility, at least for the time being."

Tanner thanked the Chief and drove back to the hotel. Since it was nearly four, he decided to put the case aside until the next day. He had a couple of hours until his dinner date, just enough time for a shower and a few minutes to sit on the balcony and soak in the noise and salty aroma of the Gulf waters.

At exactly six o'clock, Tanner was knocking on the door of the small, 1930's era house that Ginger Breedlove called home. It was in an area on the Island undergoing a restoration of sorts. New residents weren't as homogenous a group as those in other cities who returned to the downtown areas to reclaim the convenience of location. She answered the door almost immediately.

"Come in, Milo. Right on time." Ginger's wicked grin greeted him as she stepped back allowing him to enter. "Would you care for a glass of wine before we leave for dinner?"

Tanner was thinking he'd like to be invited back after dinner for the wine, but he accepted the offer. They moved into the compact living area, where she poured two long-stemmed glasses half-full of a rich red wine from a decanter.

"I hope you like Malbec," she said extending her right hand holding one of the glasses.

He took it from her, their fingers barely touching, but causing a tingle of excitement for both. "I'm not a connoisseur. I'm sure I'll enjoy it."

They sipped the wine as she told him of moving to the Island because most of her business developed in the area after Ike, the last and most devastating hurricane to hit Galveston in years. Although proud of having restored the cottage, it was not a topic that held her interest. She told him it was convenient for her work, comfortable and a good investment. Soon they finished the wine and left for dinner.

He had planned to take her to one of the more luxurious restaurants on the Strand, but once in the car, she suggested Benno's on the Beach, a casual restaurant on the seawall with a view of the Gulf. Tanner asked her about life in the real estate business and gave her a short version of his life history. She soon redirected the conversation.

"What's developing with your investigation? Still trying to send me to prison?"

Although her question was clearly asked in good humor, Tanner's response was very serious.

"I have removed you from the list of suspects. And I've convinced Molly B to let us pursue the investigation as we would any other. So except for any light you might shed on Sanford's family and acquaintances, my interest in this dinner is purely personal."

He felt the slight flush of his cheeks as he spoke, but noticed she too had a warm glow on her face in reaction to his remark.

"Why thank you, Mr. Detective. I'm glad our date is not likely to end with you driving me to jail."

When they finished eating, he drove slowly down the seawall, taking in all the early evening tourists as they gathered beach towels and umbrellas, preparing to return to hotel rooms for the night. After several blocks, he turned back into the neighborhoods and drove to her home.

"Would you like to come in?" she asked.

Minutes later they were sipping another glass of wine and talking about Sanford Hill's murder.

"Have you always felt the need to carry a pistol for protection?" Tanner asked.

"Actually, I still don't necessarily feel that need. When I dated Sanford, I went with him and Donny a few times to a shooting range on the mainland. They both decided to purchase a new pistol and Donny suggested I get one as well. Of course, the next logical step was for me to take the training and get a license. I've rarely taken it out of the house since."

"Yours is a 9mm Smith & Wesson. Is that what they bought as well?"

"All three exactly alike and with consecutive serial numbers. That seemed to be a big deal to them. Until they told me, I didn't even know guns had serial numbers." Tanner saw that grin return as she spoke.

They soon finished the wine and Tanner reluctantly rose to leave. She took his wine glass and set it next to the decanter before walking with him to the door.

"Thank you for allowing me to take you to dinner," he said.

She reached for the fingers of his right hand. "I enjoyed the evening."

He placed his left arm around her neck and pulled her to him. The kiss was long and more passionate than most first goodnight kisses. But Ginger slowly pushed him away with a hand to his chest.

"Thanks, again, Mr. Detective, we'll have to do this again."

On the drive back to his hotel, Tanner began thinking about the next date. Was he really serious about getting into another relationship? His first and only marriage ended in a disaster. His wife was unhappy living the life of a detective's stay-at-home spouse, so she'd taken a job in one of the hundreds of banks in Houston. She was smart and pretty, both important ingredients at the time for building a career in banking.

Soon she was a vice-president in the bank where she first worked and was eventually promoted to president of a bank branch.

One Friday evening, a few years after returning to the business world, she came home and announced she had met someone else and wanted a divorce. Though he was aware her interests had changed, Tanner felt blindsided. He never suspected she would leave their marriage. He first tried to talk her out of the divorce, but as the conversation developed, she admitted her new love interest was the CEO of the holding company that owned her bank and they'd been romantically involved for more than a year.

The divorce was swift and without acrimony. Tanner dealt with the pain by dismissing his now ex-wife from his thoughts. Trustworthiness had always been important in his hierarchy of values. He wouldn't live with any unfaithful woman. He knew that about himself, even if it included Ginger Breedlove, the woman who was stirring so many long dormant emotions.

Chapter 9

Thibodaux called Tanner on his cell phone at seven the next morning. "How's the trip going? You figured out how to meet up with Molly B's prime suspect yet?"

"We had dinner last night. And she's no longer our client's prime suspect. After my meeting with Mrs. Hill, she agreed that we're the experts and she'll let us do our job without interference. She'll see that family and all her employees cooperate with our efforts to find the murder weapon as well."

"Man, I called to tell you how successful I've been sitting at this computer, but it sounds like you've been busy as well," Thibodaux responded, wondering if his partner might be about to experience the same kind of life-changing relationship he had discovered with Marissa.

"I'm going to pay a visit to Donny Dragna this morning and try to start collecting some weapons for testing. But what have you learned?"

Thibodaux began with the Scardino family. "First, if any of the Scardino clan is involved, it has to be the brother Tony. The ex-wife has remarried. Her new husband has at least as much money as Sanford. The older of her two brothers, Joe, is a quadriplegic after a boating accident four years ago.

"Tony is probably not a very good suspect either, since you would assume his motivation would be to avenge his sister's mistreatment by Sanford. But that fell apart when I learned that he is involved in two lawsuits against his siblings over the estate of their parents."

"You learned all that sitting at home?" Tanner was surprised once again by his partner's ability to harvest so much information on the internet.

"That's not all. Sanford and Donny Dragna have been buying and selling pistols and rifles on Craig's List for the last couple of years. I don't know if that has anything to do with Sanford's murder, but since we're concentrating on the weapon, I figured it is worth knowing."

After agreeing they would both visit the Island on the next trip and that Marissa would accompany Thibodaux, they ended their conversation. Tanner checked out of the hotel and drove toward Hill and Sons Industries. The drive always interested him. Spaces between scattered businesses bustled with heavy equipment, working to fill the vacant land with new structures. The bayside boasted taller buildings peering over Galveston Bay. At the port, cranes steadily swung cables into and out of freighters loading and unloading cargo. Other ships cut waves through the water along the channel as they passed, heading to docks on Houston's ship channel farther inland.

When he arrived, Tanner asked to see Donny Dragna and was escorted to his office.

"Hello, Mr. Tanner. I met your partner previously. Have a seat. What can I do for you?"

"I want to ask you about the guns you own and to get a list of any that you've sold in the last six months," Tanner said, knowing that the manner of the question was likely to make the other man defensive.

But he was surprised when Donny opened a drawer and handed him a sheet of paper from it.

"Here's a list, with serial numbers, of all my weapons. Mom said you'd be asking, so I prepared it for you. I haven't sold any of them since Sanford's death, which is, I assume what you are interested in."

Tanner briefly glanced at the list of approximately twenty-five items before placing it in a folder he had brought with him. "Do you have a similar list of Sanford's weapons?"

"I'm afraid I don't, although we can look in his gun safe and see what's there, if you like. It's just next door in his office."

The two men walked to the next office, where Donny turned the dial on the safe, somewhat shielding the action with his body, so that Tanner couldn't see which numbers made up the combination. The safe contained several rifles, four very expensive shotguns, and seven pistols. Tanner pulled each of the pistols from the safe, recorded the serial number, make and model, then returned each to the safe except for three which were 9mm caliber.

He laid the 9mm's to the side after inspecting each. One was a Karr, the second a Glock and the third a Smith & Wesson. Tanner resisted the urge to look on the list Donny had given him to see if a similar Smith & Wesson was on that list with a consecutive serial number to those owned by Sanford and Ginger Breedlove.

When they finished and Donny had secured the safe, Tanner asked, "Your wife own any pistols?"

"You're certainly direct, Mister Tanner. The answer is no, she doesn't. Are you focusing your attention on my family as suspects in Sanford's murder?" His face appeared more curious than incredulous as he spoke.

"Not necessarily. Everyone's a suspect and no one's the suspect. I came to you before some others because I'm focusing on finding the pistol used to murder him. You and Sanford were interested in weapons and it was convenient to drop by. I'd like to take Sanford's three 9mm's and yours for ballistics testing." Tanner replied.

"I'll be happy to let you take the pistols you took from his safe. As for mine, I will have to retrieve them from my week-end home in Washington County. I'll be there this week-end. You can pick them up next week. Do you want them all, or just the 9mm?"

"Just the 9's."

The men shook hands and Tanner left to begin his drive back to Success. He would have liked to see Ginger again before leaving, but he decided not to push the possibility of something interesting by calling for a lunch date so soon. In a few minutes, he was driving away from the Gulf Coast with its beauty and mystery.

*****

Donny Dragna sat at his desk after Tanner left looking out the window at the busy docks across the street. He'd have to devise a plan now. Never expecting that someone would be so bold as to just ask him for his weapons for ballistics testing, he hadn't considered how he might respond. But he was an accountant and was good at rational assessment of any situation, weighing the risks, and developing a path to success with the least possibility of something left to chance.

This time, though, he'd have to bring Michelle in on his plan. After all, it was she who followed Sanford to the Seawall and surprised him when she pointed the pistol at his face. Donny could never have done what his wife did. But if he had, it would have been better planned. Now he would have to clean up after her.

It had been that way throughout their marriage. He always had to clean up her mess. It began when she wrote hot checks, overcharged credit cards and failed to make payments. Her conduct didn't make sense because funds to pay her bills were always available. Later he had to bail her out of jail when she became an abuser of prescription drugs as well as cocaine.

But the rewards made every hassle worthwhile. No Dragna had ever before occupied a position with the power and money Donny could access. When he solved this particular problem, perhaps Michelle would start listening to reason before getting herself involved in such sordid affairs again.

Chapter 10

Michelle Hill Dragna was not happy. She hadn't been since she was old enough to realize that her parents would have preferred a son to replace the child who died just after birth. Although her mother was living proof that a woman could compete in the rough and tumble world of a seaport city, her parents always viewed her as the princess destined to be taken care of by some man, preferably one whose family was from the Island.

It pleased them both when she married Donny Dragna. He was little more than a bookkeeper in a small accounting firm. But typical of Sanford Hill, Sr.'s willingness to put family first, he handed his new son-in-law the opportunity to run the finances of the family business. Donny exceeded all expectations. He understood finance, balance sheets, and made business decisions without emotion. And he was the perfect balance for a woman who showed a willingness to take risks in every aspect of her life, as most of the Hill clan tended to do.

After a year of marriage, Donny came home unexpectedly in the early afternoon and discovered his wife with her head between the naked legs of one of the company employees. The young man had been summoned to repair a pump on the swimming pool. Michelle was dismissive of Donny when she heard the door open and turned to look at him.

"Damn it, Donny. You should call before you come home. Now get the hell out of here."

The soon to be former employee wilted at the sight of his lover's husband. He grabbed his jeans, dancing on one leg as he put them on, then fled past Donny without a word.

The incident, more than any other, defined their marriage. When he recovered from what he witnessed and shook off the emotional shock, he did what he always did. Donny reverted to his accountant character. He returned to the office, called his wife's lover in, fired him and told him to leave town.

The marriage evolved into a business relationship. Donny didn't expect fidelity. For the most part after that episode, she kept her indiscretions out of their home. The two had no children and both were happy to leave it that way. Despite their lack of emotional ties, they protected each other.

When Michelle's brother began treating Donny as little more than an employee, she interceded and complained to her father. It wasn't long, however, before her husband and brother formed an alliance aimed at keeping Michelle from meddling in the decisions of the family business. But when Michelle allowed her personal budget to get out of control, or became involved in substance abuse, Donny played the part of a rescuer, always willing to bail her out of trouble.

Donny knew Sanford's murder was, in part, due to his talking too much with his wife about company business. During the month leading up to Sanford's death, the issue of taking the company public had been discussed, as it was annually when the mother, son, daughter and son-in-law discussed the future of the family business and financial future.

Molly B had no real problems with the recommendation made by Donny. Michelle was adamant that she wanted more control over the wealth that belonged to her, declaring she might sell all of her stock if the company was publicly traded. But Sanford Jr. was adamant. Hill and Sons would remain a closely-held family business. And as always in business matters which were in dispute by the shareholders, Molly B sided with her son. Although there was discussion of Sanford buying his sister's portion of the operation, they never could agree to a value or purchase price. Sanford and Michelle never trusted the other in matters of business.

Donny educated his wife about the advantages of taking the company public and she took it to heart. During a second showdown with her brother, she accused him of trying to use the company to control her life. Then, she did what Hills always did. She eliminated her opposition.

It wasn't difficult. On the night he was killed, she found him partying at a couple of his favorite hang-outs. Her plan was to follow him home and shoot him as he walked to the front door. Plans changed, however, when he unexpectedly decided to take a stroll on the beach. After shooting her brother, she couldn't control her exhilaration and rushed home to tell Donny they would now be able to disentangle their finances from

Hill and Sons Industries. Michelle exhibited no sign that the cold blooded murder of her only living brother had any emotional effect on her.

He wasn't shocked to learn what happened. Donny had witnessed her out-of-control temper in the past. Once he watched her slam their Shiatsu, Tina, against a wall, killing it for nothing more than peeing on the carpet. He had given her the dog on her birthday.

On another occasion, when they were in Houston, she had become enraged when a waitress got her drink order wrong. She threw the drink at the young woman. The glass shattered when it hit the serving tray she was carrying. The waitress suffered a rather serious laceration on her left cheek. The Dragnas settled the disfigurement lawsuit for nearly a quarter million dollars.

Donny wasn't shaken by her behavior, but as always, he counseled to move slowly. Let the police finish what they both hoped would be an unsuccessful murder investigation. Once it became an unsolved cold case, they would raise the issue of a public offering of stock with Molly B again.

As he drove home after his meeting with Tanner, Donny calculated all the possibilities regarding the issue of the pistol. Michelle suggested they throw it off the end of a pier, but he convinced her of the possibility it would eventually wash ashore. Instead, he took the murder weapon to their week-end home in the country and locked it in his gun safe. He never guessed that Molly B would hire a private detective who would ask to inspect all the family's guns.

When he explained his meeting with Tanner to Michelle, her response, as usual, was a head-on solution to the problem.

"Sounds to me like we need to eliminate the private eye," she said calmly. "But this time, you can show some balls and pull the trigger."

"Michelle, we need to think about this. Tanner isn't alone. He has a partner working on the investigation. I'm sure the investigation would be intensified by both the police and his partner if Tanner were to end up dead. Give me time to consider our options. I told him we'd have the pistol available next week."

Friday afternoon, as they drove to their home in the country, Donny came up with a plan. They would stage a burglary and report the pistol stolen. It bothered him because he knew he'd have to report other weapons stolen as well. All of them would have to be permanently disposed of. Donny Dragna did not like to throw money away, regardless of his wealth.

When they arrived at the secluded home, he took the weapons from the safe, most of them rifles and shotguns, and placed them in the trunk of his car. Then he jimmied the garage door lock and pulled the gun safe from the garage out into a field behind the house with a small tractor he kept for mowing grass.

Instead of trying to make it look as if the door had been compromised, he simply beat on the back corner of the safe until the weld broke. He learned all this by Googling "compromise a gun safe" on the Internet. He intended to dispose of the pistol in an old salt water well on the Bolivar Peninsula, once he returned home.

Donny's plan went as expected. He called the Sheriff's office and reported a burglary. A deputy arrived thirty minutes later, inspected the ripped open safe and made a report with the list of weapons Donny said were missing. He and Michelle spent the night and decided to see a movie in Bryan, Texas, just twenty miles from their country home, before returning to Galveston.

All went well, until the movie was over and they walked to the parking lot. The car was gone. Minutes after calling 911, the police arrived to take a report, but Donny said nothing about the weapons in the trunk. The officer informed them that auto thefts were on the rise and this shopping center was a particularly popular site for thieves. He speculated that most of the stolen cars were taken to Mexico. Michelle laughed when the officer joked that the thieves were in the import/export business, taking stolen cars to Mexico and returning with illegal drugs for sale in the U.S. Donny was not amused. He only hoped that the officer was correct about where his car would be taken. At least the pistol would be less likely to end up in the hands of police.

Donny could do nothing else. He had staged a burglary in order to prevent the murder weapon from being turned over for ballistic tests. But now it had really been stolen. If the officer was correct and his car was taken to Mexico before the guns were discovered, it diminished his risk by half. He would stick with his plan; tell Tanner the guns had been stolen and provide him a copy of the police report.

Chapter 11

Tanner sipped his second cup of coffee while sitting on the front porch watching a neighbor's orange-striped cat crouching under a tree, stalking birds and butterflies. He'd bought the hundred-year-old stucco house with a red tile roof in part because he liked the yard. An old Catholic Church sat across the street. When the church bells rang every Sunday morning, birds flew from all the trees. It was cat heaven.

He checked the time on his phone. Surely Ginger would be up by now. He dialed and she answered breathlessly on the third ring.

She followed the greeting with, "Sorry I'm gasping. I just finished my morning jog and I'm still recuperating."

"Hi, Ginger. It appears I'll be back in Galveston Monday. I'll drive in Sunday afternoon and was hoping you might meet me for that dinner I promised you."

"I think I'd like that. Actually, if you get here by noon, we can go to a friend's annual celebration in San Leon. He's a musician and his band will be playing. We can go from there to dinner afterward."

Tanner had hoped for a quiet afternoon with her, but was happy to hear that she wanted to spend more time with him than just for dinner. He readily agreed.

After ending the call, Tanner stood, stretched and stepped into the yard, where he played with the cat for a few minutes. Reflecting on the recent changes in his life brought a smile to his face. He felt younger than he had in a long time.

*****

When they met on Sunday, Tanner insisted Ginger ride with him. She would learn it was one of his rules. He liked the control of being behind the wheel and she didn't mind. A quick peck on the cheek and they were off to San Leon.

Tanner had never been to the waterfront community, but he enjoyed the quaint fishing village dwellings. They were less extravagant than those he'd seen on the Island, more of a working-class resort.

The afternoon was filled with music and laughter. He liked the fact that Ginger seemed to fit in with these salt-of-the-earth folks just as well as she did with the more sophisticated business world. She was a down-to-earth businesswoman, intelligent, with a knack for making people feel comfortable when around her, no matter what their social status. What he saw confirmed his previous judgment. Ginger was not a money-grubbing murderess.

Three hours after arriving, the two left and drove to a quiet Italian restaurant Ginger suggested. The owner played quiet music on a grand piano. It was a perfect place to get to know more about her.

"It's been a pleasant afternoon. Thanks for taking me to meet your friends. But I want to know more about you. Do you have family in the area?" Tanner surprised himself by asking the question.

"My daughter, Candice, lives in Clear Lake. She's a therapist in private practice. Candice is my only close family. My parents have been gone for several years."

"What about her father?" Tanner asked.

"He's remarried and lives in the suburbs of Atlanta. He's a retired pilot. His involvement with Candice has been mostly financial. He always paid his share, but never made an investment of time for her, or, for that matter, for me before the divorce.

"A few years ago, just before he remarried, he visited me to apologize for not being there as a parent. But then he said that the appeal of his new love was that she was not tied down and was free to play. At first I was angry at the comment, but then I realized that I could totally dismiss him from my life. It was liberating.

"What about you? Any children?"

"No children. A failed marriage. I buried myself in my work for years and didn't think about relationships except those business relationships I developed on the job with my fellow detectives. But I retired from that. Change is good, though sometimes difficult."

As the pianist began playing Pretty Woman, Tanner added, "He's playing your song. I'd like this dance."

He took her hand and they danced for the next hour.

*****

Meanwhile, Thibodaux was looking forward to the trip to Galveston. Marissa had enlisted her sister to watch after the nursery. She planned to spend the entire week with him. Marissa was excited about meeting Tanner's new female interest, even if he had not yet committed to an introduction. She thought he was such a private man, but Thibodaux said he was just very cautious about his relationships.

They drove to the Island on Monday morning and met Tanner at the hotel. He told them he arrived the previous day and had dinner with Ginger. Tanner was in a particularly good mood as the three ate a light lunch at the hotel. He and Thibodaux planned their week's activities as they drank coffee on the balcony.

Thibodaux agreed to interview Sanford's ex-wife, Theresa Scardino. Tanner said he would meet with union officials whose relationship with Sanford was a result of his position on the Port Commission. On Tuesday, they would meet with Molly B and collect the pistol from Donny. Tanner hoped to meet with the Police Chief as well in an attempt to convince him to have ballistic tests performed on the weapons they collected.

Chapter 12

Thibodaux drove to the address in the Jamaica Beach community where Theresa lived. It was one of the more expensive homes in the small town, located near the beach overlooking the Gulf waters. He wondered how the home had faired during the last hurricane to hit Galveston Bay, but if it had been damaged, the repairs were well done and complete.

Theresa Scardino greeted him at the door and invited him in. She led him to a large family room with windows floor to ceiling and an impressive view of the waters of Galveston Bay.

After he sat, she offered him a drink. Thibodaux thought she looked quite relaxed. In his short time as a private detective, he had learned that some people who anticipate being interviewed about a crime, even if not suspects, become apprehensive.

He declined the drink and decided to open the conversation. "I would like to ask you some questions about your ex-husband."

"I'll be happy to answer any questions I can, but let me cover some of the things that have already been asked by the police. I don't own a pistol. I was home with my children the night Sanford was murdered and both my brothers have witnesses confirming where they were that night as well."

"I understand that you did take your maiden name after the divorce?" Thibodaux asked without commenting on her information.

"I did and I kept it when I remarried, but you are welcome to call me Theresa. What else can I help you with regarding Sanford's death?"

Her tone wasn't unpleasant, but it was clear she wanted to get to the point of the visit.

"Maybe a broad question. Who do you think might have had reason to kill your ex?"

"Just after the divorce, it could have been anyone in my family. Sanford was abusive, he couldn't keep his pants on around other women, and initially he played hardball when negotiating the divorce settlement. I had no respect for him and my brothers shared my loathing, but we moved on with our lives.

"I don't know who may have actually shot him or why. As to the people I know who were capable of it, his mother or sister would be tops on my list. Those are two cold-hearted, remorseless bitches."

Thibodaux considered her statement for a moment before asking, "Any reason you know of that either would have to want him dead?"

"Not that I know of. I'm just telling you that Molly B grew up hard. I'm sure she's told you her whorehouse story. She's proud of it.

"Michelle obviously doesn't have the same background, but she lacks moral values. She screwed around on Donny, then laughed about him walking in on her. Now if she was the one dead, I'd say he would be the number one suspect, except that Donny doesn't have the guts to kill anyone. I think that may be the only reason the marriage has lasted."

Thibodaux asked a few other questions about the family and business relationships. He then thanked Theresa and headed back to the hotel. He would have some beach time with Marissa before his partner returned.

*****

Tanner spent the afternoon in conversations with union officials. Bobby Brown was the local business agent for the Longshoreman's Union. He didn't have anything negative to say about Sanford Hill. In fact, he told Tanner, Sanford was one of two Commissioners whom he could count on to listen to the union's concerns. He had no idea why anyone would want to kill him.

Brown called two other union leaders who came to his office and discussed the murder with Tanner. They, like Brown, had no ideas about the murder. One of the two, Jimmy Barnesdale, seemed nervous as he answered Tanner's questions.

When the two other union men left, Tanner asked Brown to tell him more about Jimmy. Brown grinned as the question was asked and then explained.

"Jimmy Barnesdale was screwing Sanford's sister for a while. This was several years ago. Sanford talked to Jimmy once and asked him to be a little more discreet; he said it was embarrassing his brother-in-law, Donny Dragna. That was all that was ever said.

"When we heard about the killing, Jimmy started worrying that the law would think he did it. He's a good guy except for his preference for married women. That's why he seemed so nervous. You're the first to talk to him about it. The local cops know him and about his affair with Michelle Dragna. He's not a suspect on their list.

"And by the way, if you add all the guys who've screwed Michelle since she married Donny, you're going to have a long list. No reason to make a connection that I can see. As far as I know, every man she bedded down was just about sex. None wanted anything else and neither did she."

Tanner thanked Brown and drove back to the hotel. Since Thibodaux was not in his room, Tanner used the opportunity to call Ginger Breedlove. It was a short conversation because she was closing on a real estate deal, but they agreed to meet for dinner the next evening.

When Marissa and Thibodaux returned to their room, he called Tanner. They agreed to meet for dinner at the Olympia Grill. When Tanner walked in thirty minutes later, they were already seated.

After ordering dinner and exchanging information about what they each learned earlier in the day, both were silent for a moment. Marissa took the opportunity to engage Tanner on the subject of his love life.

"So did you set another date with your new friend when you were together on Sunday," she asked with a smile.

"Not really," he responded, looking at the food in front of him. He didn't know why conversations about Ginger were so uncomfortable for him.

Marissa didn't care about his discomfort. "Tanner, are we going to get to meet her while we're here? You know we're happy for you and want to share your new friendship with you."

"Marissa, we're just friends. It's not like we're serious about a relationship. I'm not sure she wants to be that much a part of my life," Tanner's discomfort grew as he spoke.

"Okay, friend, but why don't you let her make that decision? Afraid she'll reject an invitation to meet us?"

Tanner realized she had identified one of the two reasons he was taking it so slowly with Ginger. He wanted to be sure if their relationship became serious, it wouldn't end like his marriage. He also didn't want to press her and face the possibility of rejection before it could develop. But to explain that to his friends would make him feel that he was inviting them too far into his personal feelings. He left the comment without response and the three friends walked together back to the hotel.

Chapter 13

On Wednesday morning Tanner and Thibodaux arrived at Molly B's office at seven. They did not call first, guessing she would be at her desk before any of the other office staff. Their assumption was correct.

"Pour yourselves a cup of coffee, boys," she said, nodding toward a coffee pot in the corner of her office. "What do you have for me today?"

Thibodaux took the lead. "Not much, Molly. We'd like you to tell us about your company. But first, here's what we know.

"The potential connection between Sanford's murder and the union dispute at the docks is tenuous at best. Tanner interviewed several union officials and your son had a pretty good reputation there."

"Sure he did," Molly B responded before Thibodaux finished, "he always liked to hang around the guys who actually do physical work. He thought they were the real Galvestonians. I could have told you that. What else?"

Thibodaux continued, "Theresa Scardino and her brothers appear to be poor suspects as well. None of them cared for Sanford, but they had put Theresa's divorce behind them. Besides that, they all had solid alibis. But what I want to ask…,"

Molly interrupted Thibodaux again. "Hell, I could have told you that too. Here in Galveston we have our disputes among families. Often over marriages and divorces, sometimes over business. But the people on this island are basically good, hard-working folks who love living here. I never for a minute thought any of the Scardino kids would have done this. So what do you want to know? Maybe I should be charging you guys."

Both Tanner and Thibodaux enjoyed the salty old woman's direct and earthy conversation. It was evident as both men smiled and Thibodaux continued, "Tell us about the family's concerns with taking the company public, selling stock, and creating a board with people outside the family controlling more of the decisions."

Molly B looked confused. "What's to tell? Never been seriously considered. My husband wouldn't even entertain a discussion about it, and Sanford, Jr.'s opinion was about the same."

"But it did come up from time to time, after your husband's death?" Tanner asked.

"Oh, I suppose it did. Donny always looks at every angle and lets us know about the upside and downside of business decisions."

"Did Donny and Michelle want to take the company public?" Thibodaux inquired.

"Michelle didn't give a damn about what we did with the company. She'd argue with Sanford about that and anything else he had an opinion on. But that had to do with being his little sister.

"As I recall, every time it was discussed, Donny would give us a list of pluses and minuses to going public, Sanford would dismiss it without looking at the list, then Michelle would holler and scream about him not being the only owner of the company. It would go on and on until I would tell all of them that we were going with Sanford's recommendation, then we'd move on to the next argument."

"If Ginger Breedlove didn't kill your son, *and she didn't,* do you know anyone else who might have a reason to kill Sanford," Tanner asked.

Molly B suddenly looked old and worn as she looked into Tanner's eyes and spoke, "You probably didn't think I was listening to you, but you convinced me that the girl didn't kill my boy. For the life of me, though, I can't imagine anyone else who might hate him enough to kill him. I'm beginning to think it may have been a mistake or maybe a robbery and the guy was spooked before he could take anything."

It was the first time the partners saw true vulnerability in Molly B. Both men became solemn. A few minutes later, they excused themselves and walked down the hall to Donny Dragna's office.

"Good morning, gentlemen," Donny rose to meet them as they entered his office. "I'm afraid I have bad news. My house on the farm was burglarized and my gun safe was dragged into a field and beaten with a sledge hammer until they could get my guns out. Everything's gone, including the pistol you wanted to check."

Thibodaux looked closely at the expression on Donny's face. He didn't have the experience of Tanner, but it seemed to him that Donny was more than happy to deliver this news.

If Tanner shared similar thoughts they were well concealed, "Which police agency investigated and do you have their report yet?" Tanner asked.

"It was the Washington County Sheriff's office and I asked them to send a copy of the report to me. I haven't received it yet, but you'll get a copy as soon as I have it."

As they left the offices and drove toward the police station for a meeting with Chief Barsetti, Thibodaux asked, "What do you think of Donny? He seemed to be relieved that he didn't have a pistol to turn over to us."

"Could be, but he's a smart guy. If the pistol was stolen, it may end up being recovered by the police again. Weapons are recovered more often than some other goods because they have serial numbers. So, who knows? Nothing about him makes me think he's a killer and that seems to be the consensus of others who know him."

"Oh, I wasn't thinking he's a murderer, but after talking to Sanford's ex-wife, I'm beginning to wonder if he's married to one," Thibodaux responded. "If so, it would be mighty convenient to have had a burglary just when they were being asked to turn over their pistols."

Chapter 14

Chief Henry Barsetti invited the two private investigators into his office. Once seated, Tanner got to the point of their visit.

"Henry, what do you know about Sanford Hill's sister, Michelle? Did your guys ever look seriously at her for the murder?"

Barsetti didn't appear surprised by the question. "I went to high school with her. She has a fiery personality, grew up spoiled, and lets her personal business get out on the street too much. If anyone but Donny Dragna had married her, she'd have been a divorcee long ago.

"We never ruled her out as a suspect, but there's no evidence or motive that we've found to tie her to Sanford's murder. You guys come up with something?"

"Maybe," Thibodaux began, "as far as a motive, there was a dispute between Michelle and Sanford over whether the company should be taken public. Molly was always the tie-breaking vote and sided with Sanford, but she wasn't adamant about it. She just had to go with one or the other. Looks like now that Sanford's gone, if the issue surfaces again, they'll start selling stock. That means Michelle will be a multi-millionaire in her own right and if she sells her stock, won't be tied to decisions made by the other company owners."

"I didn't know about that dispute, but what about evidence? What you've told me so far is just a theory," Barsetti said.

Tanner took the lead again and told the Chief about asking Donny Dragna to produce the 9mm pistols owned by the members of the family. Barsetti's eyebrows arched when he heard about the burglary of the weekend home and that the weapons were stolen.

When Tanner finished, Barsetti shrugged his shoulders, "Still just a theory. And if it's correct, the pistol will never be recovered because Donny will get rid of it. It may be the best theory so far, but I'm not sure where it takes us."

"I'm not sure either, but instead of marrying the investigation to that theory, why don't we start with the premise that we might still find the murder weapon. There are three cities within twenty-five or so miles of the Dragna farm. Bryan, College Station, and Brenham. Do you know whether they all have computerized pawn shop records?" Tanner asked.

"Let me check with my property crimes office," Barsetti said as he reached for his phone.

After a brief conversation he replaced the phone. "All three computerize their pawn tickets, but Brenham police are understaffed and probably slow to get the records in the computer. Give me what you have on the pistol and we'll run it on NCIC. If that doesn't get a result, I'll assign one of my guys to go with you to visit the departments in all three cities to see if we can find it."

Thibodaux sat back in his chair. A year ago, the conversation he just witnessed would have been gibberish to him. But his work with Tanner had been more than financially rewarding. It was also educational. He now knew that NCIC was an acronym for a national computer based information source. Criminals, crimes and stolen property records were all available at the touch of a keyboard.

Tanner thumbed through a file he had carried into the meeting and gave Barsetti a sheet of paper with serial numbers and descriptions of Donny Dragna's stolen weapons. He circled the number associated with the Smith & Wesson 9mm.

"I'll call you guys as soon as we run this on the computer," Barsetti said. "If there are no matches, we'll arrange for one of you to go with my guy to make a personal visit."

Tanner and Thibodaux drove back to the hotel. On the way, Thibodaux looked at his watch.

"We've still got time for a little sunshine before dinner. I'm glad you made the deal with the Hills to have Marissa make the trip with me, especially at their expense. Why don't you invite your new friend to join us for dinner?"

Tanner glanced at Thibodaux briefly as he drove, "As I told you before, I had no choice about including her in the deal. You'd have never signed on for this case if you had to leave Success without her.

"I'm having dinner with Ginger. I'll ask her if she'd like to make it a double. As I told Marissa, I'm just not sure she wants to expand her relationship with me."

"Tanner, a little optimism might help your chances. She's probably more impressed than you think. Let us know whether you'll join us."

They pulled into the parking garage and headed to their rooms. Tanner dialed Ginger's number before he reached the elevator.

Although it surprised him, Ginger was not only willing to meet his friends, she sounded excited about it. Tanner told her about his partner and mentioned that his girlfriend, Marissa, owned a nursery in Success.

The foursome met for dinner at Gaido's Restaurant on the Seawall. One of the older restaurants, it still attracted tourists and a few locals who could remember the days when a giant crab set on an iron column out front and served as a landmark for travelers.

Ginger and Marissa struck up an instant friendship. Both Tanner and Thibodaux learned Marissa worked in real estate before buying the nursery. To Tanner's surprise, he also learned Ginger loved plants and tended a garden in her small back yard. Before the meal was finished, Marissa invited her to spend a weekend in Success and offered to fill her car with plants when the weekend came to a close.

As the dinner date was winding down, Tanner received a call from Chief Barsetti.

"Sorry I didn't get back with you earlier, Tanner, but we've had a hectic day since I saw you. Two shootings and an auto accident that shut the Causeway down for two hours.

"At any rate, no luck on the serial numbers for the pistol. Swing by my office in the morning and I'll introduce you to the detective I'm sending with you to try to get more information in person from the police and the pawn shops."

Tanner ended the call as the others rose to leave. He drove Ginger home and she invited him in. After serving wine, she sat beside him on the couch. Soon they were embraced in a passionate kiss. As he fumbled with the buttons on her blouse, Tanner wondered if he should slow down. He was approaching a line he wasn't sure he should cross.

Ginger ended those thoughts by kissing his lips lightly and smiling as she released her last two buttons. Standing and taking his hand, she led him to her bedroom. Once there, Ginger turned her head and glanced toward the back of her bra. Recognizing the invitation, Tanner freed her breasts, wrapped his arms around her and gently enveloped their softness with his rough hands. He nuzzled her neck, tasting her skin and breathing in the scent of her.

Breathing deeply, she smiled and pushed him toward the bed. "I need a moment; I won't be long." She smiled walking to the dressing room.

Tanner stripped his clothes and waited in her bed. When she returned with a bath towel wrapped around her torso and slightly damp from a shower, she sat on the side of the bed. The towel fell away as he pulled her to him.

They made love three times before falling asleep, their bodies wrapped tightly together. Tanner slept soundly. He awoke early and lay with his arms wrapped around her for several minutes before gently disentangling his body. He found coffee in the pantry and brewed a pot. As he sat drinking his first cup, Tanner decided that he had just begun a new and possibly the best phase of his life. Life might be more exciting now than as a cop.

Chapter 15

Thibodaux and Marissa drank coffee in bed. He knew she would leave this morning and return to Success. Since he was likely to have a full day chasing after murder weapons in small central Texas towns with Tanner, there was no reason for her to stay in Galveston. But right now his life was complete. Thoughts of marriage never seemed to fit with his lifestyle before. But he was feeling changes to his very core. Marissa would be his wife someday soon. He was sure of it.

An hour later Thibodaux and Tanner sat in Chief Barsetti's office. They had just met Detective John Rivera who would accompany them to the central Texas towns where they hoped to find Donny Dragna's stolen pistol.

Rivera was a pleasant guy, fighting an expanding waistline with greying temples accenting a full mop of coal black hair. He appeared to have no preconceived notion about working with the two civilians. Tanner presumed that Barsetti told him enough about them for him to know they were legitimate. One a retired cop and the other a Delta Force soldier would be enough for a veteran cop. The tattoo on Rivera's arm revealed he was also a proud Marine. Thibodaux knew he would respect anyone who could earn the role of a Delta Force member.

*****

Since Marissa took Thibodaux's car to drive back to Success, he rode with Tanner. Rivera followed in an unmarked police car.

"Marissa thinks you got a real winner with Ginger, partner." Thibodaux knew Tanner would not like talking about his personal relationship, but it was clear to him that something was changing inside his friend.

"I'm glad she does. Now let's concentrate on this case. If we get lucky and find Donny's pistol, the question is whether he will agree to ballistics testing. If he doesn't, it'll be out of our hands. Barsetti's men will have to try to get an order from the court. That may be a tough sell."

"If we recover the guns without Rivera, what would keep us from firing them ourselves into something where we could recover the rounds for comparison with those found at the murder scene?" Thibodaux inquired.

The two men fell silent, each considering how they might accomplish their goal. The big problem was finding the pistols. They could work on the legalities when the time came.

The three men first called on the Bryan police, where a detective who worked property crimes searched with them through pawn tickets not yet entered into the NCIC database. No matches.

At the College Station Police Department, they learned pawn tickets were collected electronically and entered in the database almost instantaneously. Again, no matches, but a much shorter visit.

In the smaller town of Brenham, they were told clerks had a backlog of several weeks of unprocessed pawn tickets. A Brenham detective led them to a room where they were allowed to go through the four hundred tickets not yet entered in the computer system. Two hours later, they walked out, still without a match on any of the stolen weapons. They shook hands with John Rivera and thanked him for his help. He assured them he would continue to check the database in the weeks to come, waved goodbye and began his drive back to Galveston.

As they drove toward home, Thibodaux studied a map he found in the back seat. "Why'd we pick those three towns to check pawnshops?" he asked.

"Because they are close to the Dragna farm," Tanner replied.

"But what about Hempstead and Navasota? Those two towns are about the same distance, with the farm pretty much setting in the middle of all five. We're passing through Hempstead about five miles ahead. Let's check with their police department."

Tanner didn't' argue, but he pointed out that if the guns were pawned, they would be likely to end up on the national database sooner or later. Thibodaux was insistent, asking if there were any small police departments that didn't collect and enter pawn tickets in the computer. Tanner answered that he was sure it happened. Neither could have guessed that one of those towns that rarely checked pawnshops was four miles ahead and that they would get a break in the case as a result of Thibodaux's insistence.

Tanner easily found the police station, using an old trick he'd learned years before. He looked for the highest antenna tower in town, then drove to it. In most small communities the police and fire stations would be located under that tower, and so it was in Hempstead, Texas.

It was a small department with only seventeen officers, including the Chief. Tanner asked to see a detective; within a few minutes they were ushered into the bowels of the small building and introduced to Detective Jeremy Small, a last name that did not fit the man. He was close to three hundred pounds and not quite six feet tall. Tanner explained that they were trying to locate stolen weapons for a client.

"Sorry, guys. We've got one pawnshop in town. When we have an item that we're looking for, we just let Sammy know what it is. He calls us if someone pawns it. We don't collect his pawn tickets. But I'll be glad to meet you over at his place and introduce you. He'll check for your weapons. I assume you have serial numbers?"

Tanner assured Detective Small they had the serial numbers, after which they followed him to the pawnshop. After introductions, Sammy told them he might have the Smith & Wesson.

"A guy brought three pistols and several long guns in a couple of days ago. I told him what I would give him and he wasn't happy with the price. So the only one he pawned was a Smith 9mm. I still have the pistol because I have to hold it for thirty days in case he comes back to redeem it. I'm sure he won't do that, but the law requires me to hang on to it. It's a nice pistol. When I put it on display, it won't last long. Let's check to see if it matches your serial number."

Sammy thumbed through a bundle of pawn slips and pulled one out. He read the serial number aloud as Tanner and the Detective looked at the list of weapons. They had a match.

"Who pawned it," the Detective asked. "Is it a local?"

"Oh, yeah. Harold Smith. You know Harold. Him and his brothers do business with you guys regularly. Lives over on Lilac Street."

"I know him," Small said. "I'll have to take the pistol, Sammy. You guys want to follow me to his house and see what he has to say?" he asked Tanner.

As soon as they were back in their cars, Thibodaux smiled at Tanner.

"I think I'm learning this business, partner. Won't be long and you'll be asking me for advice on these investigations."

The Detective pulled into the driveway of a small frame house in a neighborhood of homes all in need of paint and repair. Tanner and Thibodaux parked on the street and followed him to the front door. His knock was answered immediately by an old black woman.

"Detective Smart. What you want this time? None my boys been actin' up agin has they?"

"Mrs. Smith, I need to talk to Harold. Is he here?"

"Oh, yeah, that lazy boy's still in bed. Let me get 'im. You knows ah don' 'low no mischief in my house."

A few minutes later, Harold Smith came stumbling through the house, rubbing his eyes as his mother prodded him on from behind. Small asked him about the pistol he pawned. He immediately became defensive, telling the detective that he bought the gun from someone he didn't know.

Tanner turned to Small and said, "Well, boss. I guess we can book him on the burglary of a residence as well as theft."

Before the detective could respond, Harold interrupted, "Burglary? Of a house? I ain't been breakin' in nobody's house. Them guns was in the trunk of a car."

He then realized he'd been outmaneuvered.

Within minutes Harold had confessed that he and a friend stole a car parked at a movie theater in Bryan. They thought they could sell it to a Mexican who shows up every month looking for cars and doesn't require a title or an ignition key. He said his friend knew the guy and he didn't ask questions. But before selling the car they had torn the back seat out and found the weapons. Thibodaux and Tanner laughed. Neither Harold nor Detective Small understood that the inquisitive car thieves had helped them capture an even bigger criminal.

"Sorry, guys. But if Harold's telling the truth, the guy who owns these guns is going to have problems greater than Harold's," Thibodaux explained. "And we're going to enjoy telling him about how we found one of the pistols. It's possibly a murder weapon."

The Detective arrested Harold and assured Tanner and Thibodaux he would send a copy of the statement to Bryan Police as well as the Galveston Department. The two partners resumed their trip home, both feeling a sense of accomplishment.

Chapter 16

Early Monday morning, Tanner and Thibodaux drove back to Galveston, planning to confront Donny Dragna. Tanner had called Chief Barsetti on Friday evening and the Chief agreed to have his detectives attempt to retrieve the pistol from Hempstead police. He would then work on getting a ballistics test. But that could take weeks. They intended to pressure Donny into making a mistake if possible.

While Tanner maneuvered through the traffic in Houston, Thibodaux's cell phone rang. It was Detective Small from Hempstead.

"I just wanted to give you guys a heads up. Your client, Donny Dragna, was on the phone early this morning. Seems Bryan police called him to tell him his pistol was recovered and that we had it here.

"He wanted to drive up this morning and get it. I told him it wouldn't be released until the court case against Harold Smith was resolved. It really upset him. He even asked that we dismiss the charges so he could get the pistol. He wasn't happy. I wouldn't be surprised if he doesn't try to have a judge order it returned."

Thibodaux chuckled, "I hope we didn't mislead you. Donny is actually not our client, his mother-in-law is. We thought that pistol might have been used in his brother-in-law's murder. I think his phone call just confirmed that. Thanks, Detective, and by the way,

Galveston P.D. will probably be calling to arrange a ballistics test."

"Already had the call. It'll be taken care of as soon as we can get it to the state lab," Detective Small assured Thibodaux before ending the call.

Once clear of Houston traffic, Tanner called Donny Dragna. He asked to meet with him upon their arrival. But Donny begged off an early meeting, protesting that he was swamped all day with business meetings and end of quarter financial reports. He finally agreed to meet after dinner at his office.

Tanner called Ginger and arranged to meet her for lunch. Thibodaux, although insistent that he would be a distraction, agreed to tag along. They met her at Paco and Rudy's, a small downtown restaurant popular with the locals. The restaurant usually had a large lunch crowd and today was no exception.

After they ordered, Ginger asked, "So what have you guys been stirring up? I got a call from Michelle Dragna just before I left the office and she asked that I meet her at six this evening. Surprised me until she said she wanted to discuss a commercial property I have listed. She's never been a client, but you never know."

Neither man had an answer for her. They didn't reveal what they learned about the missing pistol nor did they tell her that Sanford's ex-wife had fingered Michelle as a likely suspect in his murder.

There was just a hint of concern in Tanner's voice when he responded. "That's interesting, because we're meeting with her husband in his office at seven. Did she tell you what property she's interested in?"

"Yes, it's actually one we discussed several months ago. Sounded like she was a little depressed. I'll let you know how it goes if you'll call me after your meeting with Donny."

The conversation moved to more personal subjects, not the least of which was Thibodaux's suggestion that plans be made before they left town for Ginger's trip to Success for a week-end. Tanner picked the date as they sat at the table. She'd fly to Austin. Tanner would pick her up for the short ride to Success. The four could spend Saturday driving in the Hill Country, sampling the numerous Texas wineries from Fredericksburg to Sisterdale.

When they finished lunch and the conversation about the Hill Country weekend, Ginger returned to her office. Tanner and Thibodaux checked in at the San Luis Hotel where they had become recognizable by many of the hotel staff.

At six, the two partners met in the lobby of the hotel before driving to a small diner on the seawall. They wolfed down large, juicy hamburgers and then headed out for their meeting with Donny.

Upon arriving at the offices of Hill and Sons, they found the glass doors to the office entrance locked. Not having explored the remainder of the large industrial complex before, the partners decided to look for another entrance. As they approached the corner of the building, Thibodaux's phone rang.

"Go on. I'll catch up after I answer this," he said pushing a button on the phone.

Tanner walked thirty feet down the side of the building, out of Thibodaux's sight, when he spotted a metal door leading into the building. When he tried the knob it was unlocked. He stepped inside and found himself in a large warehouse with an industrial crane overhead. Crates were stacked down the center of the warehouse. He heard muffled voices from somewhere in the darkened recesses of the building.

Stepping past the last of the crates lining the center of the building, Tanner detected movement to his left and slightly behind him.

"Just be cool," he heard a woman's voice instruct him. "Don't turn around. Keep walking."

Tanner did as instructed, walking until he came to a door at the end of the building, which was propped open with a metal office chair. Stepping through the door, he was startled to see Ginger sitting in a chair similar to the one holding the door open. Terror was written like a scene from a horror movie on her face. Her hands were tied behind her and a strip of duct tape plastered across her mouth. There was more tape around her ankles and wrists.

Donny Dragna stepped from the shadows behind Ginger at the same time the person behind Tanner flipped a light switch. Although the room had not been completely dark, the sudden light blinded Tanner for a moment. When his eyes adjusted, Michelle Dragna stepped in front of him.

"You guys just couldn't let well enough alone, could you? Had to keep prying into our affairs. Well, that's alright. We're going to solve your little murder mystery for you. Problem is, you won't be around to collect your final bill."

As Michelle spoke, Tanner saw the expression of a crazed woman on her face. He had to figure out how to buy time before she did anything else.

"What are you doing with Ginger? She has nothing to do with this." He looked from Michelle to Donny for a response.

"Oh, she does now. When you came to Galveston, she was the primary suspect. She's going to die trying to keep you from arresting her for Sanford's murder. Of course, she'll get off a lucky shot first and you'll die a hero's death." Michelle smiled as she stared at Tanner.

Donny who had been silent, suddenly blurted, "Wait a minute. Where's your partner? Thibodaux was with you. Where is he?"

Before Tanner could answer, Ginger, through muffled sobs said something that sounded vaguely like, "I'm sorry, Tanner. I had no idea…"

Michelle slapped Ginger across the cheek with the pistol she held in her right hand. The hit was hard and Ginger moved her body trying to avoid it. Between the slam of the pistol against her head and her movement, the chair toppled to the side, spilling her onto the floor. Tanner's first impulse was to rush to her aid, but a quick move of Michelle's pistol, pointing it at his stomach, caused him to stop. He could see blood pooling almost instantly around Ginger's head as she lay silent.

"Donny, shoot this son-of-a-bitch, now. Don't worry about his partner. We'll take care of him when we're through with these two." Michelle was looking at Donny with disdain.

Donny hesitated. Michelle's voice was hard-edged, "Christ, Donny. You disgust me. Can't you ever act like a man? This time you better find the balls. PULL THE DAMN TRIGGER, NOW!"

But Donny Dragna was not a killer. He looked at her with pleading eyes. He found no sympathy for his dilemma in her expression.

"Michelle, let's think about this. We need Thibodaux too. If we don't finish them all, it won't work." Donny was on the verge of panic because he didn't have the nerve to pull the trigger on either of their captives. Michelle knew he wouldn't do it on his own.

Tanner could taste the bile creeping up in his throat. He knew Michelle would not let her husband off the hook.

"Donny, you're worthless. You aim your pistol at him and pull the trigger or you'll be on the floor beside him when I walk out of here."

Donny raised his pistol. His hand shook as he pointed it at Tanner's chest.

Chapter 17

Thibodaux had taken the call from Marissa just as he and Tanner were looking for an entrance to the building where they were to meet with Donny. He was on the phone just long enough to lose sight of Tanner after he rounded the corner. As Thibodaux walked in the direction his partner had gone, he found the same door Tanner had entered. Pulling it open, he heard a noise that sounded as if someone had fallen or dropped something.

The unexpected noise caused Thibodaux to enter cautiously. He could have called out to Tanner, but years of soldiering from Iraq to Afghanistan had taught him to never advertise his presence before he knew what he was facing. He began walking slowly along the wall toward where he believed he had heard the noise. He soon heard the voices of both Donny and Michelle.

As he crept to the end of the crates, concealing his approach, he saw Donny raise his pistol toward Tanner's body. Donny was focused on the target facing him. He didn't notice Thibodaux step from behind the crates. Michelle, with her back to the crates, also had no idea that he was only fifteen feet behind her.

In as authoritative a voice as he had ever used, Thibodaux instructed, "Don't do it, Donny," as he rushed toward Michelle.

The surprise Donny experienced caused him to point the gun toward the sound of the voice. He fired the pistol in a reflexive response to his excitement. But Michelle stood between him and Thibodaux. She gasped, grabbed her stomach with both hands and crumpled to the floor. In seconds a pool of blood grew around her body.

Shocked, Donny stood holding the pistol, but when Thibodaux moved the few steps to close the space between them, he made the mistake of pointing it at the veteran warrior again. Thibodaux's right hand struck his throat just below the jaw. Donny collapsed, unable to get air because the blow had partially collapsed his esophagus. Thibodaux noted a look of terror on Donny's face, but wasn't sure whether it was because of Michelle's body lying beside him or the fear that he might suffocate for lack of breath.

Thibodaux kneeled over Michelle and found her fading from consciousness. He looked at the bullet wound. The bleeding has slowed, but Thibodaux could tell from the pallor of her complexion, that Michelle was struggling to remain alive.

When the shot was fired, Tanner had rushed to Ginger and lifted her from the floor. As his partner called for an ambulance and the police, Tanner carried her outside the building. She had a nasty slash across her right cheek and both eyes were swollen, beginning to take on a purple cast from the bridge of her nose to her eyebrows. But she was alert enough to squeeze Tanner's hand just before the sound of sirens filled the air.

The scene at Hill and Sons Industries could have been a clip from a Bruce Willis action movie. Ambulances arriving, loading patients, then off again with sirens blaring; police cars, detective cars, and the Chief's car parked in the street with officers spread throughout the property; even a fire truck arrived at the scene. Tanner and Thibodaux were the only two of the cast of characters who didn't need a visit to the emergency room.

After providing a short version of what had occurred, Tanner left for the hospital to check on Ginger. Thibodaux, the Chief and several investigators would meet him there within the hour.

Upon arriving at the emergency room, Tanner learned that Ginger's injuries were not life threatening, although she would have some facial scarring to deal with later. He sat with her in the emergency room while doctors dealt with the more serious patients, Donny, and for a short time, Michelle.

"Are you up to telling me how you ended up in the warehouse?" Tanner asked Ginger.

She smiled and told him Michelle had dropped by her office and asked if she would ride with her to the offices to pick something up before going for drinks. When they arrived, Michelle shoved a pistol against her head and held it while Donny applied the duct tape.

"And that's when my knight in shining armor appeared," Ginger teased.

A few minutes later the doctor attended to her injuries and Tanner stepped out to see if he could learn the condition of the Dragnas. He went to the admitting desk where he asked about them both.

The clerk studied his face for a moment, then said, "You're Tanner. I thought you retired. I remember you from when I worked the county hospital in Houston. What are you doing in Galveston?"

Rather than explain the details and possibly be told that he wouldn't be provided information, he simply said, "No, still working, just not in Houston any longer."

The clerk made an assumption that he was still a cop and told him that Michelle Dragna had not made it after arriving at the hospital. Her husband, Donny, on the other hand, would recover from his encounter with Thibodaux's strike to the throat. Tanner resisted an urge to sneak into Donny's room and question him.

*****

By the end of the following day, Donny Dragna had confessed to his part in the murder of his brother-in-law, Sanford Hill. Once he decided to talk, he gave a detailed statement regarding every aspect of the murder.

The media went wild when they learned Michelle Dragna murdered her brother because of disagreements about the business their parents had built. The stories of her affairs and the fact she flaunted them in the face of her husband made for salacious evening news coverage for weeks following Michelle's death.

Chief Henry Barsetti, while making sure his Department got credit for the investigation, was quick to point out that the private investigation team of Tanner and Thibodaux played an important role in locating the murder weapon. Of course, their names and Ginger's were intertwined throughout the stories because of the brutal ending of which they were a part.

Barsetti met with Tanner and Thibodaux when the dust had settled, three weeks after Michelle Dragna's funeral. He thanked them for their assistance.

The Chief then asked, "Have you had a chance to talk with Molly B since the funeral?"

Thibodaux answered, "That's one of the reasons we're back in town, Chief. We meet with her this afternoon."

"She's a tough old woman, but this has taken a toll on her," Barsetti said. "Tell her I'll drop by and see her soon."

Chapter 18

When Tanner and Thibodaux arrived at Molly B's office a few minutes after two that afternoon, they were shown to a small office with a conference table centered between the door and the back wall. There were six chairs around the table. Molly B sat with her back to the wall facing them as they entered.

"Have a seat, boys," she said as soon as they cleared the doorway. "This is the room where all company meetings were held, first by my husband, then after his death, by me and my children. It's a lonely room today and I expect it won't be used much in the future. Seems as if the ghosts of all my family are gathered here.

"Sanford's children are too young to participate in decision-making and Donny will be fighting the charges of participating in my son's murder. He'll own Michelle's part of Hill and Sons, but I'm not sure he'll be around for a long time.

"One of the reasons I want to talk to you is to get your assessment of his situation. He's made bond. I tried to talk to him, but his lawyer told him to stay away from me and the business. I want to know if he was a part of the plan to murder my son or if it was all on my daughter."

Thibodaux looked at the old woman and saw the lines of stress on her face. But he didn't see any sign of resignation or defeat. As much as he might want to shift the blame for Sanford's murder from Molly B's only other child, he knew she wanted the truth.

"Donny isn't a risk-taker," he began. "I doubt he would have ever helped Michelle, or anyone else for that matter, plan a murder. He didn't give a statement to the investigators, so we don't know for sure, but I suspect that his only involvement was to help her cover up the murder after she told him what she'd done."

Molly B stared at the door behind the two investigators. They sensed that she was deciding whether to continue revealing her thoughts about all that had happened since they met her. Finally she looked from one to the other and continued.

"I've told you that I grew up hard. I'm sure you guessed that not only was I raised in that whorehouse, but I practiced the trade when I was a teenager. My husband's life was just as rough. It's why we were able to accept each other's pasts and build a good life.

"It was easier here in Galveston than it might have been in other Texas towns. Galvestonians wear their rascal nature like a badge of honor. Probably began before Jean Lafitte, but we take pride in the fact that his kind, pirates and profiteers, created what we know as Galveston. We don't pass judgment on others and the rest of Texas could take a lesson from that.

"My husband and I weren't the sentimental types, but when Michelle was born, we wanted her to be special. We tried to shield her from the raw experiences we'd had. It was a mistake. She always made sure she was the toughest kid in the neighborhood. I always knew she was thick-skinned, but never suspected she could ever become a cold-blooded killer.

"What hurts the most is that family didn't mean a thing to her. That's the part of our DNA she didn't get. The Hills always value family."

Tanner had been silent, but now he spoke, "I'm sorry for that. You've lost both your children and your son-in-law in just a few months. Try to make sure you stay connected to Sanford's kids. They'll be grown before you know it. Reach out to their mother. I think with all that's happened, she'll welcome you."

Molly B brushed aside his comments and continued, "I want the two of you to help Donny's lawyer. Unless I learn that he was involved in planning Sanford's murder, I want him back here working with me. He didn't mean to shoot Michelle. I suspect he fired the pistol out of surprise and excitement. He couldn't have intentionally shot her or you."

Neither Tanner nor Thibodaux disagreed with her assessment, nor were they surprised by Molly B's new assignment for them. She was trying to hold onto what little family she had left. Her grandchildren were not close to her, rarely having visited since the divorce and regardless of Tanner's advice, she didn't like her chances of patching things up with her former daughter-in-law.

Molly B continued, "When Donny's trial is behind us and I have a chance to digest all that has happened, I'm going to need someone to run this business for me.

"Donny can keep books, but he's not tough enough to take on the whole operation. Either of you two ever think about moving to Galveston?"

Thibodaux answered first.

"Not a chance. My days will be spent in my hometown of Surprise."

Tanner looked thoughtfully from his partner to Molly B before answering. Both thought he might take the old woman's offer.

"Molly B, I'm not interested in running a business like yours and don't have any experience with it. I do like the thought of spending some time in Galveston though. When you're ready to move forward on a new manager, I may have an idea for you.

"Thibodaux and I know a young man from San Antonio. His names Devin Blakemore. We worked a case he was involved in last year. Devin's had a rough life and I think he might be a good match for you if you decide you want a manager. We'll talk more when you're ready.

*****

It took little work to assist Donny's defense team. Any jury seated in Galveston County was likely to know of his deceased wife's reputation. Molly B agreed to testify on his behalf. It didn't take long for the District Attorney to offer a plea deal for Donny to receive a ten-year probated sentence and a ten-thousand dollar fine.

After the legal procedure was over and Donny returned to Hill and Sons Industries, Tanner dropped in to visit Ginger at her office. The facial wound had healed with not even a hint of scarring.

"It seems to me that we have a long weekend of wine drinking in the Hill Country that you promised," Ginger said, as she rounded her desk, extending both arms.

Tanner engulfed her in a hug. After a passionate kiss, he replied, "With any luck, I'll have lots of those weekends available. Now that Thibodaux found his soul mate in Marissa, I need someone to hang out with."

THE END

I hope you enjoyed Murder on the Seawall. If so, please leave a review at one of the many outlets where this and my other books are available.

You are also invited to visit my webpage at www.LarryWatts.net or email at Larry@LarryWatts.net.

Previous books in the Tanner & Thibodaux Series

Homicide in Black & White
Rich Man, Dead Man

Other books by Larry Watts

The Missing Piece
Cheating Justice
The Park Place Rangers (a book of short stories)

Harris County Public Library
Houston, Texas